A BORROWED CHRISTMAS
LOVE STORY

I0545470

A Borrowed Christmas Love Story

KATIE BACHAND

Copyright @ 2022 by Katie Bachand
All rights reserved.

Copyright ensures free speech and the creativity behind it is preserved.

ISBN: 978-1-7374434-1-4

FIRST EDITION

Cover Illustration and Design by:
Lance Buckley Design

Author Image by: Studio Twelve:52

A Borrowed Christmas Love Story is a fiction novel. Names, characters, places, incidents and plot lines are used fictitiously and are a result of the author's imagination. Thus meaning, any resemblance to persons alive or deceased, buildings, establishments, locals, or events is coincidental.

BOOKS BY KATIE BACHAND

SERIES

Taking Chances Series:
Becoming Us (Prequel)
Conflict of Interest (#1)
In the Business of Love (#2)
A Business Affair (#3)
Betting on Us (#4)

STANDALONES

Romantic Comedy:
The Problem with Love Potions

Christmas Novels:
Postmark Christmas
Waiting on Christmas
A Borrowed Christmas Love Story
The Worst Christmas Wife

JOIN KATIE'S NEWSLETTER

Head to Katie's website at
www.katiebachandauthor.com
and join her newsletter for fun content, great
deals, free books, and more.

Or, simply scan the QR code below.
(Hover your phone camera over the image!)

Enjoy!

Great Grandma Helen Tigue.

A writer of notes,
A lover of family,
A beacon of strength.

There isn't a day that goes by where
I don't long for a cup of chocolate
chips, butterscotch chips, walnuts,
and a can of Mountain Dew.

A BORROWED CHRISTMAS
LOVE STORY

CHAPTER 1

"This is Jade Conner, Cities One News, goodnight Minneapolis."

Jade angled her face just a touch to the right as she practiced perfecting her on-camera smile she would share with the city of Minneapolis.

She analyzed her appearance. Jade had applied just the right amount of make-up. Her sandy-blonde hair was perfectly molded into place – it wouldn't budge if they decided to put her on a project in the middle of a hurricane. And her welcoming grin was ready and waiting anytime she needed it.

But they wouldn't be sending her to a hurricane anytime soon. And she wouldn't need to force her smile.

Jade was about to head into her final early-morning newscast. She knew that everything she'd worked for over the last seventeen years was about to pay off.

Years of standing in the middle of political rallies, pet adoption features, her first promotion to mid-morning anchor, then to lead anchor on the morning show was all going to land her on the coveted five-thirty evening news.

Jade inhaled to the count of ten, then let it out, slowly and methodically.

This was it.

In one final, practiced movement, Jade wiped the bathroom counter and mirror and took a moment to appreciate her brand-new condo's bathroom before heading to the station. She'd splurged on the real estate – and it wasn't like her to act so brash on something so over-the-top – but she knew this promotion was coming, and she couldn't let the beautiful condo in the middle of the city slip away.

From where the condo sat, high on the twenty-first floor of the building, she could see the winter snow falling and listen to the quiet. Jade took a second to look out her window while the rest of the city slept on the cold morning. Then, just because she could, she moved to the eastern wall of windows so she could look down and see one of the many Christmas trees the city had put on display.

A twinge of guilt tried to surface at the sight of the Christmas cheer below, but she knew she couldn't think about that now.

Jade looked at her watch and saw it was quarter to four in the morning. Time to head out and get set up for their six o'clock air time. Her *last* early-morning air time.

She was about to be the face of the city's evening news. Somebody that would welcome people home from work to share the latest breaking news stories. Somebody they would make dinner with, eat dinner with. And she'd give them the best of herself.

Her dream was finally coming true.

Like so many years before, Jade switched gears as she dressed for the day. She forced herself to change from casual Jade into professional news anchor Jade.

By the time she tossed on her sleek red winter coat, she was ready to take on the city and the morning news. Except for taking a moment to pause in the doorway and turn to say goodbye to her sleek new condo, she was all business.

Nothing could distract her. Not the joyful sound of Christmas music that sang to her as she rode the elevator down to the street-level lobby, not the snow that fell around her on the streets or city trees, and not even the garland strung around streetlamps or the trees strung with white twinkle lights could take her off her game.

As she did every day, Jade stopped at the corner coffee shop. She entered, said good morning to Randy, placed a five-dollar bill on the counter, and without another word moved to the end of the long bar to wait for her drink. Randy knew her order and knew she was prepping for the show, so when the drink was ready, all he said was, "Have a great show, Jade." And that was it.

Jade absently heard Randy continue his enthusiastic conversation with his staff about upcoming Thanksgiving and Christmas plans, but she walked out briskly, not bothering with the distraction.

And, the holidays *were* a distraction.

There had been a day when she longed for Christmas. When she'd wait anxiously for the radio to change over to the happy holiday songs that she couldn't help but sing along to. For the trees and lights to go up around the city. And for that one week of bliss where she'd leave all of her responsibilities behind and travel up north to stay with her grandma and grandpa for the week of Christmas. They'd bake cookies, sing carols, take sleigh rides down to the old mill, and head into their run-down little town – which didn't have a single stoplight – and go into the shops to get gifts for the family who would join them for Christmas Eve and Christmas Day.

But all of that stopped when her grandpa passed away. And that was years ago now. So, there was no point reflecting on the bad when so much good was about to happen to her. Here. Now.

Jade finished her speed-walk to the station and swung the door open, relishing in the warmth. She hadn't realized how freezing cold it had been, but she was in the zone. She wasn't about to let her last morning newscast slide. She'd deliver her best show yet.

"Hey, Jade! Morning."

"Morning, Serena. Ready?" Jade greeted her assistant, then made sure she was ready to keep up with her on their last morning show together.

Serena waited a beat to let the seriousness of the moment set in for both of them. Then she molded herself into the mirror image of Jade's all-business demeanor and said, "Ready. Let's do this."

Jade walked as Serena followed behind, updating her on the latest breaking news. Serena prepped her on key segments she'd need to deliver with perfection, and in the end, offered a reminder.

"Don't forget," Serena said, stopping to make sure Jade was listening. "Right now, people around the world need the spirit of Christmas. They want to feel it. To love it. Make sure Minneapolis does, too."

Jade heard Serena, and she blinked. She hadn't received that kind of oddly specific reminder before. Something was up. She knew Serena well enough to know that.

When Serena stared blankly back at her, Jade lowered her brow, leaning closer to her assistant. Then, when Serena barely widened her eyes, it was enough of a break for Jade to question her.

"Why do you say that? About Christmas, I mean."

Serena hesitated, then forced a laugh and waved a hand forward while saying, "Oh, nothing. Just a friendly reminder to keep up the great work."

Jade listened to another whimper of a laugh, then looked around nervously. She grabbed Serena's arm and pulled her into the nearest, dark conference room, and said, "Okay, spill it. And don't tell me it's nothing."

The laugh and hesitation left Serena in an instant. Suddenly she was back to her sturdy, confident self.

"Come on," Jade said. "Let me have it."

Serena took a breath. "The latest numbers show our morning show dropped in the rankings."

Jade tried to navigate her way through the panic that had her palms sweating. She nodded calmly, trying not to show her nerves.

"Okay," Jade said slowly. "Okay, we can deal with that."

"That's not all."

Jade froze. Then she rolled a finger forward, indicating she was ready for Serena to give her the rest.

"There was a poll. It asked for feedback on all anchors, across all stations." Serena stopped.

"And," Jade asked, more frantically than she intended. But, really, she shouldn't worry. She'd consistently topped the list at one or two for years. What's the worst that could happen? That she'd dropped to five? That's still great.

"Thirteen."

"What?" The outburst was unintended but authentic.

The dramatic drop fell with the pit of her stomach. Jade looked down to see if she had fallen through the bottom of the floor, but she was still right there, eye-to-eye with Serena, who was a fixture in solidarity.

Thirteen?

"You're sure?" Jade needed to know this wasn't a mistake.

"I'm sure. It came in last night." Serena started to dig through the pile of papers she'd been cradling in her hands. "Do you want to see it?"

"No." Jade shook her head. "No, I can't. I need to be ready for today."

Jade tried to refocus, but she couldn't help the nagging feeling, and she had to ask. "Please tell me I'm above that scum-ball sportscaster over at *Nine.*"

Serena blinked, unmoving. Her answer, delivered with perfection in her silence.

"Really?" Jade's whisper-yell held none of her previous resolve. "He jumps – practically naked, I should add – into frozen lakes around Minnesota. He has the intelligence of a five-year-old. He *sounds* like he smokes ten packs a day."

Jade put her hands on her hips and started to pace.

Jade repeated his resume, baffled she'd come in behind him. "He jumps into ice-holes in his underpants."

"He does have a pretty good butt."

Jade stopped and looked at Serena. "So, what you're saying is, I'm worse than a man whose *only* redeeming quality is his rear-end?"

"According to the residents of Minnesota?" Serena's answer came as an apologetic squeak.

"Never mind, please stop." Jade held up her hands.

Obviously, this was a minor hiccup. One survey couldn't possibly ruin *years* of great journalism. They definitely couldn't disregard the last eight of those years when she'd executed perfect stories with perfect timing. Her emotional delivery was enviable, and the way she was able to transition from believable side conversations with co-anchors to colorful commentary was priceless.

Calming a bit, Jade rolled her head, stretching the stress-knot that had formed in her neck.

"Okay. It's okay. Everything is going to be fine." She looked at Serena. "Let's go give Minnesota one heck of a morning show."

Serena nodded. "That's my girl."

Jade straightened her slim-cut, perfectly tailored navy suit, tugged at her sleeves determinedly, then marched out of the conference room and walked right onto the set that was exploding with Christmas.

If they wanted jolly, she'd give them her best version of good 'ol Saint Nick.

CHAPTER 2

Jade beamed as her co-anchor, Adam Anderson, finished with the final feel-good Christmas piece before they signed off for the national news to take over.

"What a *wonderful* Christmas it will be, Adam, thank you."

Jade gathered herself, and just like she practiced that morning, she turned toward the camera, smiled, and delivered with effortless perfection, "Have a beautiful winter morning, Minneapolis. This is Jade Conner, with Adam Anderson at Cities One News. Goodbye."

They held the position until the cameraman's hand moved his fingers from three, to two, to one, then held up a zero.

As usual, there was a quick wrap applause – one of Jade's favorite moments of the morning – and she leaned back.

"Can you believe the amount of money people are spending on Christmas this year?" she asked Adam, who was gathering his papers. "It's just crazy."

"I'm afraid we're falling victim to the over-spending." Adam joined the small talk easily. They'd become fast friends when she joined him in the morning slot.

"Really? What on?" Jade asked.

Adam stopped and looked at her. "I just told Becky we're going to be a part of the crazy holiday travel this Christmas."

"No way! That's great. Where are you headed?"

"We are heading to Mexico. She's been wanting a warm-weather getaway for a while. Nothing like leaving Minnesota during the most wonderful time of the year. But, waiting didn't seem as exciting. So, we are heading out the day after Christmas."

"I'm so happy for you – and for Becky. I'll have to give her a call so she can gush about it."

"She'd love that. Hasn't stopped talking about it since."

Jade's smile was genuine, just like the conversation. But all of it fell away when her station manager's voice called to her from across the room.

"Jade." Melissa Corey, a ruthless, fascinating woman, stood in a festive, expertly fitted red suit. "Can I have a word? My office."

It definitely wasn't a question. Melissa meant: *You, me. My office. Now.*

Jade stared. *This was it.*

"Hey," Adam spoke quietly, so Jade was the only one that could hear. "Good luck. You deserve it."

Jade sighed and grinned at Adam, more nervous than she thought she'd be. "Thanks. Here goes."

Melissa Corey looked like an elegant statue, sitting in the middle of a fussy, over-the-top, Christmas-decorated office. Garland draped the top of the cabinets, and paper snowflakes dangled from the ceiling. A miniature Christmas tree sat on the corner of her desk, and Christmas music – though barely audible – flowed from the speakers on her computer.

It was like looking at Santa Claus holding a sledgehammer. Aggressively festive.

Melissa looked up at Jade's knock. "Jade, come in. Great show this morning. Loved your delivery on the *A City Giving Back* segment. Really great."

"Thanks – thank you, it's a great story." Jade moved into the room and began to sit.

"Oh, if you wouldn't mind closing the door."

Jade hovered over her chair, almost ready to fall in, but pushed herself back up.

Those extra squats are really paying off, she thought.

Once Jade settled into the chair across from Melissa, with only a waving stuffed Santa Claus between them, Melissa folded her hands on her desk and leaned forward, apparently giving Jade her full attention.

This was it!

Jade tried to appear casual and pleasant, but inside she was making snow angels on a puffy mound of freshly fallen flakes.

"Jade," Melissa began all business. "As you know, you have been a cherished part of this family. You've worked your way into the lives and hearts of this city for eight years as the lead anchor for our morning show."

Melissa leaned back to cross her legs and rested her folded hands on them. Like any good professional would do – on camera or off. It was the necessary buildup for an epic delivery.

It was all Jade could do to control herself. Because she didn't know what else to do with her excitement, she mirrored Melissa and crossed her own legs, hoping for at least the illusion of a poised, confident woman who'd earned the promotion she was about to receive.

"Jade," Melissa repeated her name. "We've decided to move in a different direction."

"Thank you!" Jade let the words fly out of her mouth, not bothering to comprehend what her boss had said.

When an usually overtly aware Melissa looked confused, Jade tilted her head. Then, the realization of the words sank in.

"Wait, I'm sorry. What did you say?"

Understanding flickered across Melissa's eyes as she realized what Jade had *thought* was going to happen. Then, a rare display of compassion settled on her boss's face.

"I'm sorry, Jade. I'm sure this wasn't what you were expecting."

Entering a state of shock, Jade began to tune out Melissa's voice. "No, it's not. It's my dream. Cities One is my dream." Jade looked up. "Melissa, I've worked *so* hard for this."

"I know you have. Harder than a lot I've seen come through here."

"Then, why?"

Melissa's poised self returned. It must not have been part of the discussion she wanted to have, but she was always prepared. "We are looking for something…less polished. Something...more authentic. You can deliver a great segment, but it's timed, calculated, what you think people want to see and hear. We want somebody who is just as interested in the people, and the story, as they are at ensuring what's coming across is factual and timely."

Jade couldn't believe what she was hearing.

"So, I'm just...done?" The weight of the moment hit her like a bag of coal to the chest.

"Your contract is through the end of the calendar year. Of course, we'll assist in new job placement and give you the highest recommendation between now and then. You're a fabulous journalist."

"Just not fabulous enough to keep." Jade didn't realize her thoughts had reached her mouth.

Melissa sighed. "I truly am sorry. If you need to take the rest of the day off, please do. Gather yourself. Let it sink in. We can speak again on Monday. But, Jade?"

Jade didn't know if she had the ability to speak without her voice cracking, so she hoped the look she gave Melissa did the talking for her.

Melissa nodded. "Try and use this time to think of the possibilities and the opportunities that lie before you. Change seems hard, but remember – especially during this time – it can be a wonderful thing."

Jade gave a slight nod, then stood.

Melissa stood with her, a pristine centerpiece to the chaotic Christmas backdrop. But, the contrast worked.

"We'll talk Monday," Melissa finally said.

And with that, Jade turned and walked out the door.

CHAPTER 3

The pre-Thanksgiving snowstorm gave Jade the perfect excuse to hide her face as she made her way through the aisles at the store just around the corner from her condo. She hoped the melted snow hid the tears that had been overflowing since she took her first step out of the station.

Jade had chosen a basket because she feared if she used a cart she would have filled the entire thing. There were only so many tubs of Santa's Snickerdoodle ice cream, Christmas candy bars, and holiday-themed cupcakes she should allow herself to have – even if she was catering to a heartbreak.

The cashier eyed the contents of the basket and started scanning. Then, she casually offered, "We have hot chocolate packets and marshmallows just around the corner. Or eggnog. We have eggnog, too."

Jade sniffed and sucked in a breath. "Where's the eggnog?" she finally asked, squeaking a bit at the end.

"You know," the cashier began as she sidestepped her way around the register counter. "You just stay here. Let me grab you one."

All Jade could do was nod pathetically and let the nurturing woman cater to her.

The cashier lifted the bottle to show Jade what she'd found. As if she was saying, *Honey, I've got what you need, and it's in this gigantic Christmassy jug.* Then she went on ringing everything up and sliding holiday heartbreak treats into a bag so Jade could easily carry them home.

Jade watched the woman work efficiently and appreciated her kindness. She felt terrible – like her world was falling apart – but at least she was going unnoticed.

As Jade smiled through the tiny cinched opening of her hood, she gave a breathy, "Thank you." Then she gathered her bag into her arms and started her slow, pitiful walk toward the door.

When she had almost made it back out into the bitter cold, the cashier yelled after her, "I love your morning show!"

All Jade could manage was a nod. Because the tears came out with heaving sobs. Her face was drenched. Until she walked outside. Then, all of her tears froze to her face for the rest of the walk home.

Usually, there wasn't any time for sitting around. On any given day, Jade would find herself at work, then she'd head to the gym for her afternoon workout. Around five, she'd call friends and meet them for dinner, or she'd be headed to a work event that would keep her out until seven. Then, because she had to get up at three in the morning for work, she'd head home, change into her pajamas, and settle into bed with a good book. Usually, she wouldn't make it three pages before falling fast asleep.

But now, as she sat with nothing to do but look at every beautifully crafted feature of her brand new, now extremely over-budget condo, she felt like misery was her only company.

In sweatpants and sweatshirt – because her well-fitting flannel pajamas just didn't seem to fit the mood – she sank into her couch surrounded by a tub of ice cream, an entire bottle of eggnog, and the Christmas-themed Kleenex box she'd picked up at the store with the other goods.

Jade eyed the remote through sopping eyes.

She knew she shouldn't, but she couldn't help it. After eight hours of sitting around in a condo she probably wouldn't have much longer, Jade needed something to do. And as much as it hurt, she still loved the news. So, Jade reached for the remote, pulled it close, then poked at the power button.

It was already tuned into the evening news. When she was home during the evening, it's what she watched.

Jade hugged the remote and her eggnog between her cozy sweatshirt and her knees. Every once in a while, she'd take a sip between the tears and sniffles. Then, when the screen panned to her two co-workers – no, friends – a new round of sobs exploded to the happy holiday welcome tune that played in the background.

Jade barely heard her phone start ringing through the sound of the TV and her wailing.

Rather than reach for the phone, she rolled her whole body to the side. Once her head came in contact with the decorative throw pillow that was also too much money, she looked at the caller ID.

Mom.

The readout was unmistakable, even through her blurred vision.

Jade sniffed a couple of times.

There was no way she could answer it. Her mom would be peppy, Christmassy, happy. And, she'd ask about the promotion. Why would anybody put themselves through that?

No way.

Jade's mind was made up. Until she wondered if her mom had heard the *other news.*

Jade shot up from her lying position.

Could the news of her being let go have made it around to other news channels or the media?

The idea was too much to bear. Jade accepted the call and threw the phone to her ear, hoping she didn't miss her mom's call entirely.

"Mom, hi." Jade tried her best to sound like she hadn't been crying the day away.

"Hey, Jadie. How's it going? Nasty weather out there today."

In those few little words, Jade knew that Jackie Conner – her mother and small-talk, gossip fiend – didn't know about her termination. She would have never started with her usual *weather* introduction.

Jade angled her head to look outside. Though she supposed today, during an actual November blizzard, it could have been possible.

"Hey, Mom. Yeah, the weather's terrible. And I'm…" Jade swallowed the lump in her throat, "fine."

"Oh, no. What's wrong? You had a great show this morning. Oh."

Jade listened to her mom's tone drop. And wondered if this was it.

"Did your sister call you?"

"No." Jade sat straighter. "Was she supposed to? Is Deni okay?"

"Oh yes, Denise is just fine. I thought she might have told you about your grandmother."

Jade's heart dropped.

"No, she didn't."

"Honey – Jadie – the will is to be read on Monday. The executor has requested your presence."

New tears formed in Jade's eyes, but these ones were different from the ones she'd been crying about all day. These were ones of heartbreak and hurt.

"I don't want to go."

Jade knew her voice sounded small, but she didn't want anything to do with her grandmother or the new life she'd found with a new man after her grandpa passed away.

The sigh was slight but audible through the receiver. "Jadie," Jackie started, "I know you don't want to go, but I really think you should take the next two days to think hard about it. You might never get to go back there again after this."

"Mom, I don't want to go back. I don't want to see the life that she shared with that man."

"Now, honey, don't be like that. You know as well as I do that Lenny Brock was a good man."

"No, I don't know that. All I know is that Grandpa died, and Grandma gave up the home and the dreams she built for this rich, north countryman. Like the entire previous life she had lived didn't even matter."

"Well," Jackie said the single word, then stayed silent for a moment.

Jade knew it hurt her mom when she decided to become estranged from her grandma. But it also hurt Jade too much to see her grandmother with somebody different. In a home that was completely different.

She'd gone up one time and never went back.

Every Christmas after, her grandma sent her a long Christmas letter handwritten in barely legible script. It took Jade through every detail of her grandma's new life, from New Year's Day to the following New Year's Eve.

"I suppose it would be hard for you to take the day off, but I hope you at least give it some thought. They are expecting you at the Brock Estate Monday at eleven. The weather's supposed to clear up by then."

At the reminder that she'd need to ask work to take the day off, Jade couldn't hold back her emotions any longer. Between work and her grandmother, she'd been overloaded.

"Oh, honey. I know it's so hard. It really is upsetting, but I think it's for a good cause."

"No. Mom." Jade's words were choppy and ragged. Then the next flew out on one long sob. "They let me go today."

"They what?"

The surprise in Jackie's voice was appreciated. It was the kind of scrappy disbelief that only a mother could have when somebody hurt their daughter.

"Why, I should just march down to that station and give them a piece of my mind."

Jade was grateful in that moment for her mom and the laugh that made it through her breakdown.

"Mom, no. But...thank you."

"Did they tell you why?" The rage was still present but noticeably calmer.

"That I'm not *authentic* enough."

"What does that even mean?" Jackie wasn't buying it.

"Honestly," Jade couldn't believe she was about to say this, "I think they think I don't like Christmas enough."

Silence filled the other end of the phone. All Jade could hear were the soft mumbles of the nightly news signing off for another commercial.

"Mom?"

"Oh, yes, I'm here."

"Oh my gosh, mom!" Jade couldn't believe it. She heard it in her mom's voice.

"Yes?" Her mom knew she'd been caught.

"You agree with them!"

Jade threw an angry, damp Kleenex across the room and hit the sorry excuse for a Christmas tree she'd set up before Thanksgiving. Nobody would see the condo until after Turkey Day, so on a whim, Jade had half-heartedly set it up, knowing she wouldn't want to do it the closer it got to Christmas. She scoffed at the tree and tossed another two Kleenexes in its direction like it was Christmas's fault all of this was happening to her.

"I disagree with *them*, Jadie. But I do think that ever since your grandmother remarried and you stopped celebrating Christmas with her and the extended family, you've lost a little bit of that...*magic.*"

Jade sat and let her lips fall into the dramatic frown the words of her mom encouraged.

"Mom?"

"Yes, Jadie?"

"I really just can't do this right now."

Jade listened to her mom. There wasn't a distinctive sound made. It might have been the amount of time Jackie remained quiet, or that she just knew what her mom would have done at that moment, but she imagined her mom nodding once in understanding, then taking a breath as she accepted that her girls would make their own decisions.

"Okay, honey. Just remember, if you need anything, your dad and I are just a phone call – or a couple miles – away. And, I think those Cities One folks have made the biggest mistake of their lives."

Jade's lip twitched, appreciating her mom's sentiment. "Thanks, mom. Talk later. Love you."

"I love you, too."

Jade huffed and dropped the phone to the coffee table and looked outside. It was completely dark, even in the early hour. Winter was upon them, and they were in for long, dark days. But as she watched the snow whip around outside, she let the chaos take her mind off of her problems. She'd do more crying, but she'd done enough for the day. And Jade realized because she'd never really done it before, wallowing in your own pity and bawling your eyes out all day was exhausting.

There would be time to think about her grandmother's estate over the weekend. But what Jade wanted more than anything at that moment was to sleep. So, she pulled down the throw blanket draped over the side of the couch to cover herself, and she drifted off while staring at the snowflakes outside.

CHAPTER 4

Ethan Brock tugged at his too-tight slacks and button dress shirt as he waited in his dad's office. Jeremy Brock was undoubtedly finishing a *very* important meeting that had something to do with their family lumber company.

Ethan never quite understood the seriousness of needing *wood*. Still, it had been their family's income since his grandfather started the business when he'd returned from the war – over seventy-five years ago now.

Fumbling with a miniature Lincoln Log set that sat on his dad's desk, Ethan wondered what their forced lunch would be like today.

His mom, Diane Brock, was as sweet as they came. But everybody knew, the woman who sat quietly listening to conversations, or laughing politely with friends, was the ruler of their home. And, unfortunately, that also meant she ruled the strained relationship between Ethan and his dad.

Ethan would have happily stayed up at their family cabin, consulting on projects here and there for companies similar to their own. He made just enough for the necessities in life, but he admittedly didn't need more than a place to sleep and the great outdoors, especially during this time of the year.

There was nothing better than getting up in the morning and snowshoeing or skiing before coming home to a warm cabin fire and freshly brewed coffee.

Ethan smiled at the thought as he put another log on his cabin and reminded himself that lunch with his dad was only a blip in the day. He'd be back in the comfort of the luxurious cabin in no time. Maybe he'd even get an evening winter hike in before the early dusk.

"Ethan, hello."

The startle at his dad's voice had him fumbling with a log that sent the whole cabin tumbling to the table in a crash of small wooden pieces.

Breathing deep from the surprise, Ethan closed his eyes. He didn't have to have them open to know that his dad probably rolled his eyes – or had to use an admirable amount of restraint if he didn't.

It wasn't a secret that Jeremy Brock was disappointed in his free-wheeling son. But what was Ethan supposed to do? Be miserable for the rest of his life? Waste away in uncomfortable clothing in the middle of an eight-by-eight-foot office – or worse, a cubicle?

Not a chance. Ethan shivered at the thought.

"Are you cold?" Jeremy asked Ethan as he moved to the opposite side of Ethan to sit at his desk.

"Nope. Just imagining my life in a prison-like office." Jeremy immediately regretted the words. He didn't try to be obnoxious – and he knew he was. But, sometimes, he just couldn't help it. Because the idea was literally his worst-case scenario.

Ethan watched his dad sigh and drop his head as he folded his hands and set them on the desk in front of him.

Oh boy, Ethan thought. Here we go.

Though he was getting pretty good at surviving his dad's lectures, they still took a bit of mental preparation. He had to be sure to pay attention, but only enough to hear the words – mostly so he could use them against his dad at some point – and so he wouldn't lose his cool.

"Ethan," Jeremy began, using his usual demeaning tone. "I know you don't feel like working a steady, *responsible,* nine-to-five job is the ideal way to make a living, but it's a *living.* It's a way to make sure we are contributing to society. A lot of people depend on the work we do here."

Here it was. The good 'ol wood is important *speech.*

Jeremy Brock inhaled, looking as if he was preparing himself for what came next. It was all Ethan could do to not rest his head on his dad's desk.

"Your mother and I have been talking."

That caught Jeremy's attention. Good for his dad. Mixing it up a bit.

"We've decided you have to move out of the cabin and look for a place of your own."

Just as Ethan's eyes started to wander in a different direction, they shot back to stare at his dad.

"You've decided that I need to *what?* Where exactly do you think I'm going to go?" Ethan didn't want his initial reaction to be anger, but who drops something like that on their son?

"Well, that's up to you. You can go wherever you'd like. But we think it's best if you begin moving your personal belongings out sooner rather than later. We'd like to start renting it out by the first of the new year."

"That's a little over a month away. Did you say mom agreed to this?" He refused to believe his mom would do something like this to him.

Jeremy nodded solemnly. "It was your mother's idea. She thinks – as hard as it might seem right now – that it's what's best for you in the long run."

All Ethan could do was stare at his dad. He didn't make enough money to get a place of his own. And there's no way he'd get enough business at this time of the year for a down payment somewhere.

"We don't expect you to begin this week." Jeremy Brock hesitated and adjusted himself in his chair before beginning again. "There's another matter that's come up."

"Well, that's convenient." Ethan felt himself deflate like one of those giant snowmen people blew up and placed in their yards during the holidays.

"It's about your grandfather's estate."

It was the last thing Ethan expected. "What about him?" Ethan asked, concerned. They'd only lost him a few months ago. Had something happened to the staff? The grounds?

"As you know, Helen passed away shortly after my father. As such, their estate is ready for transition. There's a will reading Monday morning. Your presence has been requested."

"It–what?" Ethan tried to absorb the information. The thought of his grandfather and his new wife hadn't even crossed his mind. He just assumed their children – the bulk of them in his dad's generation – would deal with whatever needed to be dealt with.

Jeremy continued on as if Ethan hadn't even asked the stuttering question. "The reading is at eleven. Your mother and I have arranged for a car service to drive you. We'd like to ensure you're on time."

Under normal circumstances, Ethan would have cracked a joke about who was on time for their lunch, but surprisingly he wasn't interested in making his dad's life miserable at the moment. Instead, he was more worried about his future and whatever was going to happen Monday. *And* that his parents assumed he needed a ride.

"I can get there myself." Ethan decided that was confirmation enough that he would go and that he wouldn't need a car service.

"Eleven. In the morning," Jeremy repeated the time as if Ethan assumed it might have been at night.

"Right. Amazingly enough, I got that much. You know," Ethan stood. "I'm not actually that hungry at the moment."

Ethan watched his dad's shoulders drop.

"Ethan," Jeremy said. "We really are doing this because we think it's for the best."

"Right, you said that already. Tell mom 'hi' for me."

Ethan walked out of his dad's office without another word, feeling his dad's stare at his back. He didn't turn around until he reached the stairs. He paused once, letting his head fall back. Then he moved through the door and headed for the cabin.

By the time Ethan had gotten back to the cabin, it was past the time where he could go out for a hike or a quick ski. And he desperately wanted to work off some of the built-up anger.

Instead, he moved inside and made himself a grilled cheese sandwich with a bit of ham on it and heated up a nice hot chocolate. It's what he would have had with his grandpa if they had been together on a cold night like this one.

Ethan let his mind drift to the cabin, where he would live, and how much money he had in his savings account. Admittedly, what he considered *broke* wasn't really what most people thought of when they heard the term. He hadn't needed much. He'd been living in the cabin free of charge. So, he had a nice little nest egg.

But, when it came to what a new house or apartment would cost, he definitely didn't have enough money for *that*. Not if he needed the first month's rent or a small down payment...and then was expected to keep making payments.

He was lucky when he considered the reality of his situation. But, if his parents wanted him out after Christmas, he was going to need to act fast.

Chomping on his sandwich, Ethan made his way to the wood-burning fireplace and put a little kindling under the stack of wood he'd prepped that morning. It lit quickly, instantly battling the chill that had taken over the room while he was gone. He crouched by the flames until there wasn't a crumb left on his bearded chin or his fingers.

Without standing, he reached for his hot chocolate that he'd set on the side table and took a sip. Usually, he would have settled himself into the leather chair next to it and thought about where to adventure next. Would he explore a new section of their family's land, or would he enjoy a good old-time record while he sipped a hot drink and read the day's newspaper?

Tonight though, Ethan laid on the floor next to the fire and stared at the ceiling. And, every once in a while, he lifted his head and awkwardly sipped his hot chocolate before dropping his head to the ground again.

When his phone buzzed twice in his pocket, he decided the cabin wasn't quite remote enough. Even though it was more like a chalet, that didn't mean his network speed and cellular reception needed to be top-notch.

Ethan pulled it out and saw the readout.

Mom.

Of course, she'd reach out after a day like today. His dad would deliver the hard news, and she'd reach out to console.

He swiped at the message and read the text aloud. "*Ethan, don't forget, your dad always has a place for you at The Brock Lumber Company. And, we love you.*"

That was it, huh? Well, maybe his dad hadn't been lying. His mom must be in on the eviction.

Talk about a lump of coal for Christmas, he thought.

Maybe he needed something a little stronger than hot chocolate.

The thought made him think of Monday when he'd take the trip to his grandfather's estate. He loved visiting Grandpa Lenny. He was always ready with a quick quip and a laugh.

Admittedly, it had been hard when his grandpa told the family his intention to remarry. In fact, Ethan felt guilty for not stopping by during the early days. It had been so hard to see him with somebody other than his grandmother.

Over time though, he'd come to enjoy the brief, passing conversations he'd had with Helen, but he was never interested in more. He never wanted to let her in.

Going to the estate now, during his grandfather's – and his – favorite time of the year, would be difficult.

Ethan was going to have to do himself a favor and visit his grandfather's den and treat himself to a parting gift to help him get through the next month.

After an hour of thinking and watching the fire fizzle out, Ethan decided there wasn't any use trying to keep himself awake. Holding his eyes open had become a chore. And, if he were honest with himself, sleep was a lot easier than dealing with his unfortunate reality.

Ethan's hands found his face and rubbed up and down the length of it as he let out a groan.

"Merry Christmas to me," he grumbled just before he rolled onto his stomach so he could push himself up off the floor.

As if on cue, his phone buzzed again. He eyed the screen.

Mom.

Ethan flicked it open and read.

One last piece of advice. Don't put this off. Make a decision, and act. You can do it!

Ethan blinked and looked around the room. "Does she have a radar or something?"

After he shook off a combination of irritation and a bit of fascination, he turned his phone off.

Not bothering to change out of the long johns he had thrown on when he got to the cabin, he scratched his belly, then his beard, and fell into bed.

He'd be productive...tomorrow.

CHAPTER 5

"Knock, knock! Anybody home?"

Jade heard her sister, Deni, call from the entry of her perfect condo. The beautiful, meticulously detailed, wonderfully modern, but effortlessly cozy condo – that would soon no longer be hers.

The realization came to her the first time she woke up in the middle of the night. So, at two in the morning, Jade crunched the numbers. She determined that after all of her payments, she would have two – *yes, two* – months where she'd be able to pay her mortgage.

"What in the–?" Deni stepped into the expanse of the condo's exclusive open concept living room and took inventory of everything she was seeing.

Jade rolled her head over the back of the couch and watched Deni look around while she discarded the winter gear that had probably helped her survive on her walk over. Four blocks were a lot when you were battling whipping winds and snowdrifts between the city's high-rise buildings.

First, it was a cream-colored knit hat, then a bright red jacket, followed by gloves that held no fashion value at all, but they kept Deni's fingers warm and attached.

"Jade, what is going on in here?" Deni asked the question while she eyed the kitchen sink and counters that were littered with empty ice cream cartons, half-eaten bowls of popcorn, and cheap Tupperware and paper bags from the takeout Jade had been eating for every meal.

"Be nice to me," Jade said. "There's a blizzard out there. Nobody should have to go outside in a blizzard after getting fired from their job."

The last words hitched, and Jade placed her head back on the couch and shoved a Kleenex into one of her nostrils.

When Deni moved into the living room and stood between Jade and the TV, her eyebrows lifted. "Wow. Mom said it might be bad. But I didn't think it was college-boyfriend-break-up bad."

"This. Isn't. College. Boyfriend. Bad." Jade had to say each word with a careful breath in between each one. Then her lip quivered, and she lost it. "This is worse. This is all of my hopes and dreams. This is like finding out Santa Claus isn't real, you know?"

Jade squinted in disapproval as Deni pinched a smirk away.

Through blurred vision, Jade pointed a drenched tissue at her sister. "Learning that Santa Claus isn't real is like learning you've been living a lie your entire life. It makes you question everything – what to believe, who to believe, it makes you wonder if *you* ever really believed." Jade looked down, remembering the moment she realized she'd been lied to year after year. "It's a terrible, awful, dark place. A place where Christmas mornings don't exist."

Jade's eyes lifted and locked with Deni's. "It's a place like this one."

Deni waited ten seconds. Then put her hands on her hips. "Okay, great. You're at the bottom. Are you finished now?"

Jade threw her hands and head back, showing her exasperation. "And I need to go to that monstrosity that Grandma moved into when she married Lenny."

"Ah," Deni sounded like she'd been waiting for it since she walked in. "There it is."

Jade sniffed and lifted her head to look at her sister. "Mom told you about that, too?"

"Of course she did. The rest of us grandchildren just got a nice, hefty payout."

Jade shot up. "What?"

Deni grinned. "Thought you might like that."

"Try the opposite of *like*. So, you get the Mercedes, and I get a lump of coal?"

Deni moved her head back and forth, exaggerating how much thought went into calculating a more accurate number. "More like four Mercedes." Then Deni wiggled her eyebrows and added, "The expensive ones."

This time, rather than yell, Jade stood and threw all of her snot-filled Kleenex at her sister in rapid-fire succession.

"That is not fair! You get money, and I get to show up to the worst place on the planet."

Deni's laughter as she dodged the Kleenex assault wasn't a welcome one.

Jade looked around for something else to throw, but she wasn't willing to lose the chocolate sauce or the cookie dough log with Rudolf's picture in the middle.

"You'd be more upset at *you* for that one than at me," Deni said, having watched Jade's eyes travel to the raw dough. "We both know it's your favorite."

Jade wasn't giving in, but she softened. "I know. You're lucky."

"And, Jade?" Deni said, risking a step forward. "Grandma and Lenny's home is the furthest thing I've ever seen from *the worst place on the planet.*"

Jade slumped her shoulders and whimpered. "Can we pretend? Just for a day, that it is?"

Deni moved all the way in and wrapped her arms around Jade. "Sure, Jadie. Today, it can be the worst."

There wasn't much to clean, considering most of the mess around the condo was garbage. But after lugging the bags up and down the hall to the elevator, then hauling them over to the building's garbage bins, the girls were tired, sweating, and hungry.

"Since I'm avoiding the inevitable, the truth, and other quite serious things, we should probably keep my unhealthy food streak going. Want Chinese?" Jade asked from her end of the couch. Each lying head to toe.

"Mmm, Chinese." Deni slapped at Jade's foot. "And hey, I'll buy."

Jade sighed. "I want to hit you, argue with you, and tell you that's a real low blow. But I'm broke. So, I need you to buy. I've already overspent my weekend's rations."

Over Chinese food, in the middle of Jade's impeccable floor, the girls talked and watched the latest holiday dating show on TV. Jade had wanted to turn on the news, but Deni took the remote from her and told her she wasn't willing to sacrifice her enjoyment of dinner to watch Jade sob her way through the news.

"So," Deni stole a glance at Jade, who was twirling noodles in her takeout container. "You're going to go, right?"

Jade lifted an eyebrow without looking up. "I'm assuming you mean the reading of the will?"

"You always were so clever."

"Funny."

Like she usually did, Jade had weighed the pros and cons of going to the reading to an exhausting measure. Meticulously noting every possibility, outcome, and everything in between – right down to the clothing she'd wear if she went. But the bottom line, the ink, was that her grandma had abandoned her family, and she couldn't live with that.

"You know why I can't."

It was the one area of their lives that they disagreed on. Jade thought their grandma had written them off, and Deni was happy their grandma didn't have to spend the rest of her days and nights alone.

"Then," Deni said, "you know why I don't agree with you."

"It's different for you."

"How?" Deni challenged Jade where she would usually let it slide.

Jade took a big breath in, thinking of all of the ways and reasons why she felt left behind. And, though she wasn't ready for the feeling, or the words, her exhaustion got the better of her. "Because she left me for him."

When Jade's lips quivered, Deni took her in. And there it was, finally. The truth as Jade knew it – as she felt it.

"Okay," Deni comforted. "That's enough for tonight. Okay. Let's just watch the show for a little bit."

They talked late into the night about everything. Work, their parents, friends, and secret crushes – from celebrities to Jack Frost. Both of the girls admitted that if Jack Frost was real, he'd be a total babe.

Finally, they'd made their way to the bedroom, each curled into their side of the bed. And Jade fell fast asleep for the first time all weekend, grateful that Deni had stayed with her.

The following day – *Monday morning* – Jade woke to the sound of Deni shuffling around her room. She rolled to her side and tapped her phone.

"What the?"

Squinting the sleep away, Jade sat up and watched Deni navigate the dressers and closet with the flashlight from her phone.

"Denise, what are you doing? It's five in the morning."

Then it hit her. *It was five in the morning.*

"Oh my God! It's five in the morning! I overslept!"

Jade shot out of bed and lunged for her phone but missed it as Deni pulled it out of her reach.

"What are you doing? I'm late for work."

"No, you're not."

"Yes, I am! Give me that." Jade faced Deni in a stand-off.

"You are not late for work," Deni said, finally.

"I am supposed to be there...thirty minutes ago."

Deni paused, hoping the frantic panic would subside. She motioned for Jade to breathe with her by inhaling and raising her hands up and down with each breath.

"Stop that," Jade ordered, not buying into the calmness.

"Fine," Deni gave in. "I called your boss."

"You *what?*"

"I told them due to a family emergency, you were unable to go in today."

"We don't *have* a *family emergency.*" Jade glared at her sister and added, "Yet."

"Oh, come on, like you really wanted to go in anyway. Besides, you're almost all packed for a day trip."

"Lovely," Jade faked a pleasant response. "Where am I going?"

"You're going to the will reading."

"No, I'm not."

"*Yes*, you are."

"Am not."

"Are."

"Not!"

Deni looked around the room as if something in there could give her an idea. A spark of blackmail or a hint of false hope Jade could cling to.

Jade watched her sister look around, following her eyes as they traveled the room. First, across the hardwood floor, then up the smooth walls to the tall ceilings, and to the expanse of windows in nearly every room. Then she watched Deni's eyes flicker.

The wicked gleam in them made her look like an evil snow queen, about to ruin Jade's day.

"What if you learn you also inherited a sleigh-full of money?"

Jade knew where Deni was headed, and it was going to be a low blow. "Don't say it."

"What if going meant you could keep your condo? *And* not have to jump at the first job thrown at you. What if you could stay here *and* wait for the next perfect anchor position?"

Jade finally took that breath. She put her hands on her hips and tapped an irritated foot. She hadn't calculated that angle. It hadn't even crossed her mind.

Jade looked at Deni, who was grinning as if she knew she'd won.

"You knew you were going to do this the whole time, didn't you?" Jade asked, accusing her sister of falsifying her weekend niceties.

"I did," Deni admitted, "But, to be fair, I didn't know what exactly I was going to use to get you to agree."

"I haven't agreed."

"Yet," Deni corrected. "You haven't agreed *yet.*"

"You're feeling awfully confident that I'll change my mind."

"Because I know you."

"What does that have to do with anything?" Jade had to admit, she was a little curious.

"It has everything to do with this morning. If you wanted to go, you'd have to go now. Grandma's is five hours away. You'll stop to pee, grab snacks, a large fry from Micky-D's, and that will give you just enough time to get to the reading by eleven."

Jade blinked.

Deni added, "No time to think about it. Just have to act."

"This is cold and calculated."

"Thanks!" Deni beamed.

"Not a compliment."

"I'm taking it as one. Oh," Deni said the word like she just remembered the most important part. "I pre-ordered your coffee at that place around the corner. Everybody knows you have to start a wintery morning drive north with a good coffee."

Jade looked around the room. She saw her weekend bag packed and zipped, her purse sitting next to it, and her boots propped against the wall. When she looked back to Deni, she noticed Deni was holding clothes in her hands.

"What are those?" Jade nodded toward Deni.

Deni smiled and held out her hands. "What you're wearing today."

Deni really had thought of everything.

Jade watched the wall clock tick into another minute. If she wanted to make it, she really would have to leave now. And if it meant she might be able to keep her place – her glorious luxury condo – *maybe* it was worth it.

"Fine."

"Fine?" Deni questioned with too much surprise. Then she repeated, "Fine! You're going." Deni slowed. "Okay, you're going. Let's go. Here, take these."

Deni handed Jade the fitted jeans and oversized turtleneck sweater she'd picked out – perfect for the drive and formal enough for the reading.

As Jade dressed, Deni set out her toiletries, lining everything on the counter so Jade could use them before she tossed them into her travel bag.

Jade applied just enough make-up to cover the bags that two and a half days of crying had formed below her eyes and added a little color to her cheeks. She brushed her teeth, patted on some lip gloss, and lifted her sweater to lather on thick coats of deodorant. Finally, she piled her hair on top of her head and twirled it in a circle, so it sat in a giant bun.

Jade and Deni assessed Jade's appearance in the mirror. Jade was less than impressed, but Deni cheered.

"Near perfection!"

Jade rolled her eyes as she left Deni behind in the bathroom.

"What?" Deni asked.

"Like you needed to say, *near.*"

Deni laughed a bit, then followed Jade out of her bedroom, through the living room, and down the long entryway. Deni dropped the bags at her feet when Jade turned and gave her one last look.

"You're not coming down with me?" Jade asked, hoping her encouragement would walk her to the car.

Instead, Deni gathered her up into a big hug and squeezed a bit of confidence into Jade. Then she mumbled into her sister's sweater. "No. Somebody has to stay behind and clean up our mess. It'll be ready for you when you get back home."

Jade squeezed extra hard. "Love you, Denise Helen."

"Love you, too, Jade Jaqueline. Now, go save this condo. She's a real 'beaut."

Jade waffled a little in the entry. Deni pointed to the clock. "You're going to be late. Go, now." Then she smiled.

Jade gave a hesitant laugh, then nodded. "Here goes. Better be worth more than a lump of coal."

CHAPTER 6

Jade sat outside the iron gate at the end of the long driveway and stared at the massive European-style countryside home. She rested on the steering wheel and let her gaze follow the line of the snow-covered decorative spruce trees. The drive had already been plowed, and it created a snow-hedge that trimmed the drive toward the house.

The shutters and door frames were bordered in snow as well. The picturesque beauty of it all had Jade thinking of how much she would have loved driving by this house at Christmas if she didn't know who it belonged to.

Jade checked the clock and saw that she had five more minutes before she'd be late. She was *never* late. And since she'd come this far – all five hours of the drive – she might as well go in.

But, she supposed she had two more minutes to compose herself.

Jade moved her forehead to the top of the wheel and closed her eyes.

"In and out. Just get *in* and *out.*"

Jade's mantra was interrupted by a loud bang and the most obnoxious sounding vehicle she'd ever heard. She looked up in time to see an old, white monstrosity bramble by her at a speed too fast for snow-covered streets.

Then she saw the driver.

"No. Way." Jade's jaw dropped as she let the disbelief fall out of her mouth.

She shifted her car into drive and sped down after the rusting white Jeep. The wheels spun out of control, slipping and sliding her car down the narrow lane.

Slowing enough to avoid a collision with the rusty bumper, Jade threw the car in park and shot out of the car as she watched the man exit his.

Jade slammed her door to get his attention, and when he turned, she saw that he felt just the same about her as she did him.

"Oh, come *on.*" Ethan took one look at Jade and dramatized his displeasure at seeing her. He rubbed a gloved hand down his face and over his beard in a low growl. "What are *you* doing here?"

Jade eyed Ethan up and down, assessing his disheveled, unkempt appearance. She hated that even though he looked like he just got attacked by a polar bear, he was still good-looking. He was the kind of guy who was long and lean, so every grubby piece of clothing he threw on was still attractive. And, Jade assessed, tiredness only seemed to add to the sharp angles of his face.

Blushing at her own weary appearance, the only response Jade could think to give was, "Did you even shower?"

"Only on days when I feel like I'll be running into the evil Snow Queen."

Jade narrowed her eyes at Ethan but wondered if he got the reference from *The Chronicles of Narnia*, the intricate children's book she used to read with her grandma, or if Deni had called ahead and given him the reference.

"Ah, I see you two have already found each other and are getting along wonderfully."

Jade and Ethan turned their heads toward the steps of their grandparents' house.

"Good morning, Sully."

Jade whipped her head around at Ethan's greeting toward the man, then watched him try and be funny.

"Jade and I go way back. Far back enough for me to know that she's a stuck-up rule-follower, who forgot she had a grandmother who loved her." Ethan smiled like he'd just given Jade a compliment rather than gouged her with a pointy candy cane.

Sully's chest visibly rose and fell. "I can see this is going to go just about as well as I assumed." He turned toward the door. "Please follow me."

Ethan took a step aside and obnoxiously motioned his hand forward. "After you, Snow Queen."

Jade shoved her purse under her arm and took a determined step. When she felt the bottom of her boot give way, making that first terrifying slide on slick ice, her eyes grew wide, knowing the inevitable crash to the cold ground was about to follow.

Before she hit the ground, she felt two hands loop beneath her arms, catching her right before she landed on the ice.

Did he really just save her from a painful fall to an ice-coated cement?

Jade didn't know what to say through the embarrassment or the lingering scent of chocolate and caramel on Ethan's breath.

What did he eat this morning?

She felt him lift her easily, then watched him move around her while he spat new irritating words over his shoulder. "Couldn't let your ice-cold heart shatter before you even got inside."

Jade's jaw dropped. Then she stammered as she searched for some kind of retort. *Thank you* was definitely out of the question, so she found herself speechless. Irritated, confused, and speechless.

When Ethan was safely inside the door, and he couldn't witness her slow movements toward the steps, Jade tentatively slid one boot at a time in the direction of the door. Then, she carefully used her hands to steady her body on the steps as her feet made the climb to the top.

Jade didn't see the man who Ethan had called Sully waiting for her at the door. If he was bothered by waiting, he didn't show it. He just stood, silently, as Jade thanked him for holding the door, then watched her move through it.

As she entered the house, a wave of Christmas memories swirled around her. First, the one and only Christmas she'd spent in the house she was standing in now. Then, all of the times Jade had spent with her grandma at the humble home her grandma and grandpa had shared together.

Not wanting to be the cause of further delay, Jade began the act of removing her boots while she looked around.

She'd forgotten how grand it had felt but how warm and cozy it made her feel. Jade hated that even for its size, the massive country home still felt inviting. *That* definitely had to be thanks to her grandma.

There were five choices she could have made upon entering. Straight ahead of her, Jade could go up the winding banister of stairs or continue down a long hall toward the kitchen, grand dining room, and living area. Or she could go left or right. Left would take her to the den and bar, or right would take her to the library and sitting room. But the limiting options didn't do the expanse of the space justice.

"Ms. Conner?" Sully's voice sounded far away as it pulled Jade out of her thoughts.

When she looked in his direction, he didn't wait for a response.

"This way, please."

Sully ushered Jade to the right toward the library.

The walls were lined with books from the floor to the ceiling, and the sight had her heart aching as she took it in. Her grandma had loved to read. If she had to choose a favorite room in the house, this is the one she would pick. She loved this one because she knew it would have made her grandma the happiest.

Jade spotted Ethan as she moved all the way in. He wasn't seated in either of the wingback chairs or on the long couch that faced the fireplace. Instead, he was leaning against the edge of a hand-crafted bookcase on the opposite side of the large executive desk. His arms were crossed, and he was leaning casually, with one leg carelessly crossed over the other at his ankle.

Jade felt herself flush again, so she looked away.

She wasn't surprised at her reaction to him. First, he'd humiliated her upon introduction to Sully, then saved her from what was sure to be a painful fall. Of course, the demeaning attention would fluster her.

But, she had to admit, if he hadn't been a lazy, misguided, irritating man – or the grandson of the man that stole her grandma away from her – she might find him appealing.

"Please take a seat," Sully said, guiding both hands to the chairs sitting opposite the desk.

Sully organized the papers resting on top and slid thin glasses to the tip of his nose. He looked over the documents and blinked. First at Jade, then at Ethan.

When both hadn't moved, Sully ordered, "Please, just sit down. You can get on hating each other when we're finished."

Jade felt she needed to take the high road. "I don't hate him," she said, moving toward the chair closest to her.

"Nope," Ethan began to cross in front of the desk. "She just thinks I'm as worthless as an empty stocking on Christmas morning."

Jade contemplated the assessment. An empty stocking might not hold much of anything inside, but it was still pretty. As far as comparisons went, it was actually very accurate.

For nothing other than her irritation, Ethan crossed all the way to the other side of the desk, avoiding the chair closest to him, and instead took the chair that Jade would have naturally gone for.

Jade rolled her eyes and wordlessly moved to the remaining chair.

"There, we've done it." Sully looked visibly relieved. "Now, shall we get down to business?"

Both Jade and Ethan nodded.

Sully happily accepted their agreement. "Great. You both know why you're here, yes?"

Jade moved forward in her chair, prepping to ask a question.

"Here we go," Ethan said, rolling his eyes before Jade could get started.

She slanted her eyes at him. "I'm sorry for wanting to know *why* you and I are the only ones present for this reading. Obviously, my grandma and Lenny had more than two grandchildren. None together, but it begs the question, don't you think?"

Ethan just mocked her silently, mouthing, *obviously.*

The loud, exhausted sigh from Sully proved he was already growing tired of the children bantering. It had the necessary effect – for the moment – as both Jade and Ethan refocused and moved their attention back toward him.

"Jade, to your question. The rest of the estate was handled solely through monetary payments. All prepped for disbursal upon your grandparents' passing."

Sully searched his papers and pulled an envelope out of the stack, and lifted it. "This," he motioned to the white triangle, "was to be delivered the Monday of the week of Thanksgiving. Which is why we are here today, months after the passing of Lenny and Helen."

Jade only nodded. She didn't realize, or maybe she didn't want to think about, how much talking about her grandma would tug at her heart. So, when tears threatened, and she saw Ethan watching her, she quickly lifted her head and tried to show some resolve.

At the sound of the envelope opening, Jade saw Ethan's attention move back and focus on Sully, allowing the breath she'd been holding to exhale quietly.

"Are you ready to begin?" Sully asked, looking from his paper to Jade and Ethan over his thin glasses that still hung on the cliff of his nose.

Not knowing if she'd be able to speak without her voice cracking, Jade heard Ethan reply.

"Yes, we are."

We are? Jade thought. *Interesting.*

"Good." Sully didn't give Jade the time to think about Ethan's words. "Let's begin at the top." Sully cleared his throat. "As the executor of the Brock estate, I am responsible for carrying out the deceased's wishes as laid out in their trust and will."

Sully paused, looked up, then back down. "I'll just dive right in. *It is our decision, Leonard and Helen Brock, to leave the entirety of the land owned by us, 124 acres, and the business that lay thereon, to both Jade Conner and Ethan Brock. It is our decision to also leave the house – in full – and responsibility of the staff who are employed there, to both Jade Conner and Ethan Brock.*"

Neither had noticed the other, but as the text was read, Jade gaped with her mouth hanging open, and Ethan slid down into his chair, covering his mouth in shock.

Sully continued to rip off the Band-Aid.

"The ownership shall be divided equally, giving each person one-half ownership of the land, business, buildings, and house. The transition will occur on December twenty-six after both of our passing, and only if the following criteria are met."

Jade blinked and looked at Ethan to see if he heard the same line about preconditions. She watched Ethan pull himself forward and rest on his knees. It looked like he'd been paying attention.

"Are you ready?" Sully asked, peering over his glasses.

"I don't understand." Jade shook her head. "Any of it, really. It's too much. But, did you also say that criteria had to be met?"

"Yes, Ms. Conner. Are you and Mr. Brock ready for me to read the stipulations?"

Jade looked at Ethan, who already had his eyes on her. She tentatively nodded, and he did the same. Then they nodded once more in Sully's direction.

"Good," Sully said, removing the top page of the text he was reading.

"Jade and Ethan must do the following beginning the day after Thanksgiving, through Christmas Day. Jade and Ethan must follow the requests explicitly, or the prior listed lands, business, and house will not fall to their ownership, and other directives for the estate will follow.

"First, Jade and Ethan must eat every meal together when they are both on the premises of the residence.

"Second, dinner must be eaten together every night – regardless of location.

"Third, Jade and Ethan must decorate the house and grounds for Christmas.

"Fourth, Jade and Ethan must do one outdoor activity together each day, until December twenty-three.

"Fifth, Jade and Ethan must familiarize themselves with the lumber yard located on the south side of the land. They must walk or drive to the site at least two days per week.

"Fifth, Jade and Ethan must eat breakfast in town at least one day per week.

"Finally, Jade and Ethan must join each other in the den or library every night during their stay and read the materials left for them in their bedrooms."

Sully took a breath, then removed his glasses and rubbed the divot between his eyes.

"Now," he started. "Do you have any questions?"

Jade felt like a reindeer in headlights. How does somebody even begin after hearing something like that?

"So, we have to move here for a month without being able to leave?" Jade asked, with what she thought was the most obvious clarifying question.

"Really? *That's* the question you have?" Ethan asked through a quick laugh.

Jade saw the humor in his eyes. "Yes," she defended her question. "Some of us have jobs."

"They do?" Ethan asked, looking like he knew more than Jade wanted him to.

"Yes," she said firmly.

Ethan appeared to already be ignoring her and asked a question of his own. "Who will be monitoring our activity?"

Sully nodded. "As the property's caretaker, I will be monitoring and assisting with your activities – though, only if it's requested of me."

Ethan nodded, and Jade thought she could literally see the wheels turning in his mind.

Finally, Jade asked a question she figured Ethan might actually find helpful. "How many days do we have to decide?"

"If you wish to fulfill the prerequisites to your ownership, you *both* must arrive here, at the house, no later than five o'clock in the evening, the day after Thanksgiving. In addition, each of you must be a participant in the activities. Should one of you decide to not participate, it forfeits the ownership for the other. Is that part clear?"

"As clear as a slow freeze of ice on a lake." Ethan nodded.

Jade looked at him, shaking her head, wondering what that even meant.

Ethan leaned toward her, knowing she was lost, and whispered, "When water freezes slowly, it freezes clear. The conditions have to be *perfect* for it to happen."

Huh, Jade thought. That actually made sense.

"Do either of you have a strong feeling one way or the other about your participation in the prerequisites?" Sully looked from Ethan to Jade and back again.

Surprising both of them, simultaneously, Jade and Ethan said, "Do we have to answer?"

CHAPTER 7

Jade looked like she was making a snow angel in the middle of her parent's living room floor, with her arms and legs stretched out wide. The cute knit Thanksgiving sweater she'd decided on that morning was making her too warm, and she'd unbuttoned the top button of her fitted jeans for a bit of breathing room.

When she felt – and heard – Deni walk into the room, she groaned.

"Are you moaning because you ate too much or because you still haven't decided if you're going to accept your *Christmas Challenge*?"

"It's not a *Christmas Challenge*. It's a list of stipulations that need to be upheld – or executed – for *both,*" Jade rolled her eyes as she emphasized the word, "Ethan and I to inherit the land and buildings that used to belong to our grandparents."

Jade paused for a second, then added, "But yes, I'm also so full I think I'm only going to go back for one round of dessert instead of two."

"Did you unbutton the top row?" Deni asked as if it was known that more food would fit underneath you if you made more room in your pants.

"Yup."

"Cider-five!" Deni handed her sister one of the apple ciders she brought into the room, and they clinked them playfully.

Another day of eating too much turkey, stuffing, green bean casserole, scalloped carrots, and mashed potatoes. And my gosh, did they have sweet potatoes too? Then, of course, there was the dessert. Apple pie, pumpkin pie, and Robert Redford – the delectable chocolate and cream layered dessert. Dang it, she might have to go back twice.

Was there any day better than Thanksgiving?

"I know what you're thinking."

Jade rolled her head to the left to look at Deni, who had stretched out next to her on the floor.

"Bet you don't," Jade replied, sounding like they were four years old.

"Christmas is better." Deni looked Jade right in the eyes.

"Okay, maybe you do." Jade considered it a loss. "How is it better?"

"Please tell me you're joking."

"No way."

"Um, I'll start from the outside and work my way in. Snow. The snow literally turns our life into a winter wonderland."

"It's *literally* snowing right now."

"Fine. Lights. Lights go up everywhere, and it's magical. Then there's the tree. All of the ornaments from our lives – mine are better."

"We all know mine are better. Continue." Jade made sure to keep Deni on track.

"You get all the same delicious food, except the desserts are exceptionally better; for example, the wide variety of cookies. We get to see family. Then, there's Santa Claus."

"You are too old to count the man in the red suit."

"Fine," Deni hedged. "Then I'll give you one word: Presents!"

Jade laughed. Deni was still a kid at heart, and Jade loved it.

"You're such a child."

"No, I'm fun. And come on, you have to admit it. Thanksgiving is nothing but an excuse to eat a lot of food. It's like it's trying to be Christmas, but it's not."

"I'm pretty sure it's a day we're supposed to be thankful for all that we have," Jade said, acting like the older, wiser sister.

"Well, in that case – you should hate Thanksgiving." Deni tried to shift the topic. "Because you can't be thankful for your job, and you definitely aren't thankful that you have to go spend the next month with Ethan. Though, he *is* a total hunk. I think I was only fifteen when I saw him last, at the funeral, but that's all I needed. Heartbreaker, that one."

Jade rolled to her side and rested her head on her hand. She took a sip and started her defense. "First, I don't even know if I'm going."

"It's tomorrow."

"I know. Second," Jade wasn't willing to dwell on the timing, "There's more to looks than a too-tall, lanky frame, and those face lines that you see when he smiles."

Deni grinned. She knew Jade thought he was cute, too. "Like what?"

"Like, for instance, the fact that he lives off of his parents."

"I would totally do that if our parents were rich."

"You would not. Stop that." Jade reprimanded Deni by setting her cider on the floor and flicking her arm. "He's also grubby. It doesn't look like he showers or shaves. His clothes make him look like he's trying to live off the land. He might even sleep outside. And that *Jeep*. It looks like the abominable snowman growling and banging around as he drives."

Jade could picture it perfectly. In fact, she remembered the entire scene from Monday perfectly.

"So, are you going?"

"I just told you, I don't know."

"I think you should go. Remember why you're doing this."

"I know." Jade sighed and fell back again. "Condo, car, lifestyle. It will be a nice hold-me-over until I can find a new job that I love."

"Jeez, did you turn that into a mantra?" Deni asked, laughing.

"Yes. Yes, I did."

"Good for you. Now, let's go get more dessert. Then we'll make mom give us lots of leftovers so we can have it for breakfast tomorrow."

"We?"

"Duh. I'm not letting you pack for this *Christmas Challenge* by yourself. Besides, I need to be there when you change your mind thirty times tomorrow morning about going."

Jade contemplated and finally nodded. It was probably pretty close to what would happen. "Okay. But it's not a *Christmas Challenge.*"

"Whatever. Let's just go make you a millionaire."

The next day, four and a half hours north, Ethan was tossing what clothes he had from his closet into a big duffel bag. He wouldn't need much. There was a washing machine and dryer on his side of the house – assuming he'd be staying in the room he usually claimed when he'd visited his grandpa. Besides, he was going to need more space for all of his outdoor gear and equipment. He was thinking snowshoes, hiking boots, snow boots, and a couple different snowsuits.

The decision to stay at his grandpa's house for the holiday season wasn't a hard one. But, the caveat that he had to stay there with a beautiful, pretentious journalist – no, *news anchor* – was tough to swallow.

They'd never gotten along.

They'd crossed paths once when his grandpa and Helen first moved in together. Then once more, at their funerals. He'd followed up on her a couple times, thinking she'd been cute when he first saw her. But the blonde hair, preppy blushed face, and tidy looks were all a façade for the cold heart and forced laughter he saw on TV. She was practiced and polished. Everything *he* wasn't.

Ethan looked at his watch and saw that he had an hour before he was due at dinner. Plenty of time to get there before the deadline. No doubt the Snow Queen was there already. Or, maybe just to hand it to him, she wouldn't show up at all.

With the Jeep loaded up, he shoveled away the snow that had fallen after he'd gotten back from his parents' house after Thanksgiving.

The day had been...interesting. He loved seeing his aunts, uncles, and cousins. But, his mom and dad were chilly toward him, and he to them.

He had to admit, it was a little hard not feeling sorry for himself – especially when his dad was hyping up to all his relatives that they'd made the decision to rent out the family cabin.

By the time he was done shoveling, Ethan knew he better hit the road. He jumped in the car, turned the engine, then listened to it clank a couple of times before petering out.

"Not now, baby. You can do it. Just one more drive. C'mon," Ethan willed the car to start.

When it didn't, and it made the same sickening sound, Ethan looked at his gages. He didn't know *why* he looked at them; they hadn't worked in a couple of years now. But it felt like the responsible thing to check.

Ethan jumped back out into the cold and went through all the checks. Why try and guess when you could save time by shooting through all of the things it *might* be?

He threw some gas in it, checked the oil and added a fresh jug, popped the hood to check all of the connections, then wiggled his way into the snow so he could pull himself under the Jeep. No leaking.

Well, might as well give it another shot.

Ethan hopped back into the driver's seat, closed his eyes, and turned the key.

"Beautiful purring engine, that's my girl."

Ethan closed the door and prayed he'd make it to his grandpa's house by dinner.

CHAPTER 8

Jade sat at a vast dining room table intended for twelve. At first, she was there alone, so she had wandered the undecorated halls before moving into the dining room to ensure she was on time. There, she waited another half hour for Sully to arrive. When he did, he held two plates with tin cloches over them. Jade guessed it was their dinner, and the covers were for keeping it warm while they discussed what came next.

If anything came next. Jade looked at her watch and to the doorway once more.

"We'll give him five more minutes," Sully said while he organized a stack of papers into two piles in front of him.

Jade nodded, feeling anxious about what she was getting herself into.

Three minutes, two minutes, one minute.

She couldn't believe it. He wasn't–

"I'm here! I'm here!"

Jade and Sully looked toward the door, where they heard yelling coming from a distance.

"Well, holy–"

"Nutcrackers?" Sully offered the alternate phrase ending for Jade.

She nodded absently, accepting his preferred word. "Sure, whatever you want to call it."

All of a sudden, Ethan lunged into the room, tumbling in like an avalanche. Jade and Sully jumped at his surprising entry.

He was dirty and sweaty. And if Jade wasn't missing something, he looked…in total disarray.

"Ethan," Sully said after his initial surprise had passed. "Glad you could join us."

Ethan nodded, looked around, then pulled out the chair with the second place setting. "Glad I could be here."

He looked like he meant it as he sucked in a breath and rested a hand on his knee to try and gather himself.

"Okay." Sully looked over his glasses as he had earlier in the week. "We know the rules. I've printed each of you your own copy. Your first dinner is tonight. It's been prepared for you. After tonight you'll have to prepare your own meals."

Sully pulled off his glasses and folded them in his hands.

"I suggest you use tonight to plan out your week. There aren't a lot of requests, but each requires its own amount of time, attention, and planning. I won't hover, but it's a small town; make sure you're doing what's been asked of you, or it'll get back to me."

Jade nodded, and out of the corner of her eye, she saw Ethan do that same.

"Lastly," Sully stood. "I encourage you both to try and *enjoy* your time here. Take pleasure in the season. I know Lenny and Helen would have done just that. It was their favorite time of the year. They made it very special for their friends and family."

Sully nodded one last time, then moved around the table and out the door, leaving Jade and Ethan alone. Neither of them said a word, so when Sully had finally opened and closed the front door, both heard the echoing sound, then looked at each other.

She couldn't help herself. "What happened to you?"

Ethan smiled. "Car trouble."

"I can't believe that rusting snowball even runs."

"Maybe we could eat before you start throwing icicles at my face?"

Jade smiled pleasantly. "Of course."

The heavenly scent of sweet potato pot pie filled the air as they lifted the silver domes from their plates. Each had their own little pie, steaming in a rustic-looking ramekin.

Jade grinned at the sight but looked up when Ethan started laughing.

"What is it?" Jade couldn't help but hold her smile.

"Grandpa's favorite meal. For as long as I live, this smell will always remind me of him."

How could she say anything sarcastic to that?

Jade looked down, appreciating the sentiment, and fiddled with the rust-colored napkin before neatly placing it on her lap.

"Oh my gosh," Jade moaned after her first bite. "This is delicious."

"You're not lying. Can you cook?" Ethan asked, sucking in quick breaths from a bite that was too hot.

"I can, but I've never made something like this. Can you?"

"If it's meat you're looking for, I'm your guy. I'm also decent at soup. I can throw together a cold-cut sandwich. Everything else is a little questionable."

Jade gave a slight nod. "Looks like we won't go hungry."

After a few minutes of dining in silence, Jade reached across the table and grabbed one of the paper stacks. She looked at the requirements bulleted on the first page.

"Grandma wasn't messing around," Jade said while flipping through the rest of the pages quickly, but without thoroughly reading them. As far as she was concerned, the front page was all that mattered. If they couldn't make that happen, it was all for nothing anyway.

"I agree with Sully," Jade said, satisfied that she had all she needed. "I think we should plan out these first couple of days until we get the hang of having to coordinate schedules."

"Sure." It made sense enough to Ethan.

"So, for our first day, I think we should–"

Jade said, *Send Christmas party invitations out* at the same time Ethan said, *head to the lumber yard.*

She looked him in the eye. "People need to have time to *plan* to make the trip here. We aren't exactly close to civilization. And this could change a lot of people's plans."

Ethan slid his stack of papers to the right of his plate. Nodding to the text, he said, "It says we have to go twice a week. It's already Friday. We have to go tonight and tomorrow. Otherwise, we already lose the game."

"This isn't a game." Jade hated that he was right.

Tonight, Jade thought. There was nothing she wanted to do *less* than go out into the freezing cold that evening to go look at a vacant lumber yard. "Fine. Should we go in the morning?"

"We could hike there. It's not too far. You'll see on our way over tonight. It would cross our daily activity off the list. Then you could have the entire rest of the day to avoid me." Ethan moved his head from side to side. "Except, obviously, for lunch, dinner, and bedtime stories."

Jade felt like she wanted to cry. But, she admittedly had done enough of that.

"Okay." Jade set her napkin on the table next to her half-eaten dinner. "I think I'm going to try and settle in before we meet in the den. Should we come down around seven?"

Ethan nodded. "Sounds good to me, Snow Queen."

"Quit calling me that. I'll see you in an hour."

"Hey," Ethan said quickly before she made it out. When she turned, he asked, "You're not going to eat that?"

Jade rolled her eyes. "It's all yours.

Ethan laughed as he reached over to her plate to lift the now lukewarm dish. As he took heaping bites, he thought to himself, *this might not be half bad.*

CHAPTER 9

In the time he had between dinner and seven o'clock, Ethan hauled his bag up the stairs, claimed his bedroom by plugging in his phone charger next to the bed and tossing his bag on the old dresser, then gave himself a nice long, hot shower.

He threw a pair of lounge pants and a t-shirt on, and as he pulled the shirt over his head, he noticed the box in the middle of the bed.

Walking over to it, he looked inside and smiled at the sight.

An old, tattered copy of *A Christmas Carol* sat on the very top of a pile of Christmas books he remembered reading with his grandpa growing up.

Ethan sat on the edge of the bed and pulled it out.

Carefully, he thumbed through the pages, looked at the rips and scratches years of use had given it. He sniffed it once and let the stale smell of paper fill his memory of times he'd never get back.

His grandpa was the only one who seemed to understand him. Lenny even encouraged him not to settle for doing anything he didn't genuinely enjoy.

"Oh, Gramps. If you could see me now. I wonder if you'd still feel the same?"

Ethan closed the book and slid it under one arm. He grabbed a sweater and started to make his way down the stairs.

The house wasn't decorated yet, but he knew that was on their list of things to do. Admittedly, he was a little excited for the chore. He hadn't seen many places that looked like this one when it was decked out for the holidays.

Ethan made a mental note to hunt down the Christmas decorations as he stood in the doorway of the den and flipped the switch to his right. With it, only two soft-light lamps came to life, offering a moody, subtle glow. It was peaceful. Fitting for the darker accents in a house filled with European creams.

Like he had the other times he'd made his way into the den, Ethan started by moving around the room toward the old radio. He flipped it on and grinned when he realized it was already tuned into the local station that had started their holiday tunes. Then he made his way around the sitting chairs and knelt in front of the fire. He set the book on the side table behind him and got to work.

There was no use in either of them being uncomfortable. And a fire added a sort of nostalgic feel to the home. Plus, he liked working with his hands. So, he expertly piled a stack of wood in the hearth, then lit a match and watched it come to life. It didn't take long for a robust blaze to snap and flare as the heat consumed the logs.

Ethan knelt by the flames for a while and let the wandering thoughts of his life take over. It was something he'd never blinked an eye at. But now, it was always one thought away. The questions of: How did he get to this moment in his life? Had he really not enjoyed anything enough to try and make it an honest living?

Even the Snow Queen had a passion.

Ethen pushed off of the floor and moved toward the small bar in the corner of the room. It held his grandpa's favorite bourbons and whiskeys from around the world. There were bottles of wine lining the shelves and in a cooler beneath the counter. But all of that seemed too...serious. After all, Thanksgiving was over – *thank goodness* – and he needed something a little more festive. Ethan turned toward the island and opened the mini-fridge hiding beneath it.

There it was. Christmas's gift to everybody. Eggnog.

Ethan poured two crystal glasses full and moved back toward the fire to wait.

Upstairs, on the opposite side of the house, Jade had settled into one of the pretty guestrooms she'd remembered from her time spent there years ago. It hadn't changed. Every simple, lovely detail had frozen in time.

Jade took the time to appreciate it while she moved her clothes into the intricate wardrobe and placed all of her toiletries into their rightful place in the powder room. She stored her suitcase in a small closet, then closed the door and turned.

Two boxes were resting on the bed. Jade saw them when she'd walked in. But now, the thought occurred to her that she had chosen a bedroom that must have been intended for her.

Sitting on the bench at the end of the bed, Jade picked up the first box. The outside was decorated with Christmas trees, reindeer, and little Santas. She placed it on her lap and opened the top. Inside, a small ceramic light-up Christmas Tree was resting on a bed of garland and twinkle lights.

Tucked beneath the tree was a little envelope. Jade pulled it out, opened it, and read it aloud.

"A little Christmas magic for your room. Use as you wish." Her voice was quiet as she read.

Jade set the note next to her then looked around.

Without thinking, Jade set the box next to her as well. She reached inside for the little tree, put it on her bedside stand, then plugged it in. When she did, little multi-colored lights came to life.

A small, happy laugh bubbled out, and Jade wondered if she had enough time for more. She stretched across the bed to where she had dropped her phone and saw she had twenty more minutes before she was due in the den. And really, would she rather spend the time here making her room a little more festive or go downstairs to be with a man who was sure to cause the *opposite* reaction in her than the tree did seconds earlier?

The decision was made. Jade rolled to the end of the bed, scooted off, and pulled the garland out, reaching high with her hand, then grabbing more with the other. With the garland draped in a long rope, Jade turned and looked at her room. She first eyed the wardrobe, then the window, but as her eyes skimmed the room, they stopped and tracked along with the frame of her four-poster bed.

It was perfect.

Jade crawled onto the bed and flung one end of the garland over the top of the bed. Then she continued catching and tossing the end until she'd draped the first strand the length of the beam. She jumped down and grabbed another, repeating the action. Then she did the same with the twinkle lights.

When she was finished, she stood with her hands on her hips, grinning from ear to ear at the pretty way it looked. Now, all she had to do was...plug it in.

"Hmm," she hummed.

No extension cord. Well, she could find that downstairs.

Not wanting to leave her room, even though she was getting close to her cut-off time, she decided she could use her last couple of minutes to look inside the second box.

Jade set the Christmas box on the floor, then sat in the same spot on the bench, and this time pulled the old box onto her lap.

It looked like it had been opened thousands of times. The old, thin cardboard box was curling at the edges and had layers of tape holding together torn corners and rips from years of wear and tear.

Gingerly, Jade lifted the delicate top from the box and set it upside down on the bed behind her. When she turned back, she saw what must have been more than fifty letters folded neatly, sitting upright like they were in a file folder.

Jade fingered through the first couple, then pulled one out.

It was worn and ragged. The edges were yellowing at the creases. She turned the envelope over and saw the postage was dated: *December 24, 1948.*

Jade let the date sink in, and her eyes grew with wonder.

"Three years after World War II ended," Jade whispered.

Her fingers meticulously and carefully lifted the flap of the envelope and pulled out the letter. She saw that the date at the top matched the one on the postage, then skimmed down the old messy cursive to the end. When she read the salutation, she sucked in a breath.

Always Yours, Lenny Brock

Jade quickly closed it as she heard the distant chime of a grandfather clock. She placed it gently on the top of the other letters and tenderly replaced the cover.

She started to run out of the room, but the shock of what little she read had her pausing in the doorway. Jade took one look back at the box that had been waiting for her.

Was this what she was supposed to read with Ethan in the den?

Jade looked down. She didn't know what was in those letters. She wasn't ready to read them herself, much less share them with a stranger.

Jade made her decision, took one step backward, and closed the door behind her.

As the last chime sang out, Jade sprinted the final stretch toward the den. She stopped abruptly when she realized Ethan was there waiting for her.

Jade stood listening to the soft holiday music that was playing. She heard the snaps and felt the warmth from the fire that had been lit. And when her eyes found Ethan, he was leaning forward, reaching for a glass of eggnog.

"Already drinking, I see." Jade couldn't help it. When she was around him, she was compelled to irritate him. Probably because he irritated her.

Ethan stayed silent.

Jade watched him stand with the glass in his hand, navigate the chairs and tables, walk up to her, and offer her the glass.

"Oh," she said, not wanting to be ungrateful, but it had been surprising. "Thank you. Sorry, I just thought…you know? That it was yours." Jade rolled her eyes as Ethan walked away for how ridiculous and formal she sounded.

Just as she was settling into her shame, she heard Ethan say, "Don't be. I've been drinking without you." Ethan looked at his watch. "For a good half hour."

This time, Jade's eyes made a loop out of annoyance.

As they settled into their own chairs – Ethan leaning back, resting his ankle on his knee, and Jade pulling her feet beneath her – Jade saw a weathered book sitting on the table between them.

"*A Christmas Carol?*" she asked.

Ethan swallowed the sip he'd taken and nodded. "It was sitting on my bed. I'm assuming it's our reading material."

Jade nodded once, keeping the details of what was left for her to read to herself. She wasn't good at keeping secrets, so she opted to change the subject instead of feeling awkward and guilty.

"Should we discuss ground rules and expectations for the next twenty-five days or so?"

Ethan took another sip. "If it would make it so we didn't have to have this discussion anymore after today, *yes.*"

Though annoying, his agreement was better than nothing, Jade supposed. So, she chose to ignore his banter. The sooner they agreed on the outcome of their unfortunate short-term situation, they could reach the long-term goal. Then each could go their separate ways with their half of the inheritance.

"Okay," Jade began, knowing she had to make the first move, being the responsible one. "I'll make my suggestion, then you can make yours. We'll discuss until we can agree on a single scenario."

Jade finished and took a sip of her eggnog. Her eyes brightened, and she looked up.

"Wow! This is *really* good."

She took another sip, keeping her eyes on Ethan, who was watching her. If she wasn't mistaken, his annoyingly attractive lip twitched up in a quick grin.

"My grandpa used to make it homemade. My guess, actually, by taste, I know it's the same. Somebody must have made it and stocked the fridge."

"I hope we don't run out." Jade meant every word. "This is the *Happy* in Holidays*!"*

"Okay, Snow Queen. Let's talk about expectations before I change your name to *Lush.*"

"That's not nice."

"Ah, so now you know how I feel with every word you say to me."

Jade lifted her nose. "Humph."

She didn't know what else to say. And was that feeling...*shame?* She wasn't really that mean to Ethan, was she? *Mostly,* she was saying something to get a rise out of him…wasn't she?

"Come on, don't start beating yourself up now. We've got twenty-five days of Christmas for you to make it up to me. So, let's have it."

Jade sat, giving him a blank stare.

Have his eyes always been that deep chocolate-brown? Were they the exact same color as his hair? Fascinating.

When she noticed Ethan's eyebrows raise, a silent question as to what she was staring at, Jade blinked and cleared her throat.

"Right." She pulled her legs closer and took one more sip.

"Obviously," Jade began. "We don't want to co-exist in this place once our penance has been paid."

"Obviously," Ethan agreed.

"So, I think we should agree that we will sell the house – offering it to family first as the right thing to do. And figure out how to manage the land that the business is using. It's my guess that it's zoned for business use already."

"It is." Ethan knew that much having listened to his dad talk business in passing. Or directly to his face. But he'd come away with the same conclusion.

Jade was intrigued that Ethan had known something about the work he tried so hard to avoid.

"Great," she said. "Then we accept we'll have to work together for as long as it takes to complete any necessary paperwork once this is all finished?"

"Works for me." Ethan lifted his glass, moving it halfway between himself and Jade.

The surprise of the action had Jade fumbling her almost empty glass to meet his.

When they clinked, Ethan said, "To an uncomplicated, fifty-fifty split."

"Cheers." If nothing else, it was a good excuse for Jade to polish off the last few drops.

Catching Jade off guard again, Ethan reached out his hand. When she did nothing but stare in question, he motioned her to empty glass.

"Oh, right. Thanks." She watched him, perplexed at how nice he was being. "Why are you being so nice to me?"

Ethan laughed easily. He removed the cork from the large glass jug the homemade eggnog was in and poured. "Believe it or not, I don't really know how to *be* anything. What you see is what you get."

"So, you being nice to me means you're actually nice?" Jade didn't believe it.

"If the Christmas clog fits."

Jade appreciated the saying. "That's actually clever." She blinked, looking away. "I think I just gave you a compliment. Maybe I should stop the eggnog."

She looked up to see Ethan standing before her with two glasses refilled. "So, should I just?" Ethan pointed back to the bar, asking if he should take it away.

"No! No." Jade waved a hand toward her body, then left it out to wait for him to hand it over. "I want it. It's delicious."

Jade brought it to her lips and looked over the rim as Ethan settled back into his chair. He reached for the book on the table and replaced it with his eggnog.

"Are you ready?" he asked, holding up *A Christmas Carol.*

"Do we just read it?" she asked, wondering when it was the last time she'd had somebody read aloud to her. Which was funny, because really, she read aloud to people every day. But this felt different.

"I don't mind reading if you don't mind listening."

Ethan's comment surprised her. For some reason, she assumed that he wouldn't like reading. Her presumptions about him were starting to seem a little off. And, she didn't know if that sat well with her. She liked him in that little pocket of her mind where she could find him adolescent and annoying. Not bookly and nice.

Jade listened as Ethan started reading. She couldn't help but grin when he started with the title page, reading first, *A Christmas Carol,* then the author, *by Charles Dickens.*

Ethan's voice sounded gruff, deep. But the way that he read easily and fluidly mesmerized Jade. Before long, all Jade noticed was the warmth of the fire, how comfortable she felt snuggled into the oversized chair, and the beginnings of a cherished, classic Christmas story.

CHAPTER 10

It had only been an hour since he started reading, and for most of it, Jade had been awake. She'd been looking at him but not really seeing him as she listened to the words of the story and let the images play out in her head. Or, he'd see her profile, with her head resting on the side of the chair as she gazed into the fire.

This time, though, he looked up and saw her eyes had fallen closed. That was not good.

Ethan didn't want to wake her up. In fact, he felt the urge to grab one of the throws tossed on the side of the chair and cover her with it.

She looked pretty, peaceful. It was his new favorite version of her. Beautiful and silent.

Grinning, Ethan knew he couldn't leave her. They had things they needed to do. And, as much as he didn't want to throw on his boots and toss on a jacket, they at least had to drive out to the lumber yard so they could check it off of today's list.

"Hey." Ethan rubbed the top of her hand. "Jade."

Jade didn't move, but her eyes flew open. "I'm listening. I'm awake."

Ethan laughed. "Very good. But, I'm sorry to tell you, that's not good enough."

"What do you mean?" Her voice had a bit of dread to it.

"We have to drive to the lumber lard."

"No." Jade dragged out the word in an exaggerated pout. "That might very well be the worst thing you've ever said to me - or possibly ever will."

"C'mon, Snow Queen. We have to do it. It'll be quick. Get your boots, jacket, hat, and mittens if you want them. I'll drive. Just give me your keys, and I'll do the rest."

Ethan watched as Jade slowly turned her head, an evil Grinch-like, curling smile forming as it moved.

"Why do you need *my* keys?"

Ethan shook his head at her tone. "The abominable snowman died."

"Ah, so that's why you were so late and disheveled."

"I was not disheveled. I was dirty and sweating and maybe smelling a little bit like oil and gasoline. But *never* disheveled."

Jade pinched her lips and nodded. "Well, I *am* sorry to hear about your loss."

Ethan watched her pull her feet out from beneath her and stand. "No, you're not."

"Yeah," she said, now openly smiling. "You're right. It was really terrible."

"That's not nice. Old Abominable and I have been through a lot together."

Ethan followed Jade out of the den toward the entry, where Jade began rifling through her bag.

"Here," she said, tossing her keys in his direction. "Do you know how to find this place?

"Oh yeah. I used to sneak away and go watch the big, cool machines when I was little."

"Such a boy."

"Every bone," he admitted.

They dressed, putting on their winter gear in silence, and when they finally stood, sweating from head to toe, Ethan asked, "Ready?"

"Let's go before I melt."

"I think that's the other witch," Ethan joked.

"Ha-ha, very funny." Jade punched his shoulder playfully.

The instant they stepped outside, they began to steam. The heat escaped from their bodies, and Ethan wondered if there was any better feeling than that? The feeling of cool, crisp, fresh winter air. It tasted and smelled so clean, so pure.

"Really in your element, aren't you?"

Ethan opened one eye and angled his head to look down at Jade, who had been watching as he relished in the winter weather.

"Yes, I am." He didn't think it required more detail than that. So, he trotted down the stairs, used Jade's fob to unlock the doors, then climbed in through the driver's side door.

Winter at night was arguably Ethan's favorite time of the day during his favorite season. He liked the dark. It didn't bother him like it did some people. Instead, he found it peaceful and quiet. He liked the black backdrop for all of the white snow. Then when the moon or an occasional light hit the snow just right, he thought the way it kind of glittered was as close to magic as the world could ever get.

"What are you thinking?"

Ethan stole a glance over at Jade while he drove them down a quiet road. In any other season, they would have felt the bumps from the gravel, but with snow plowed and packed down, it was a smooth ride.

"I was thinking I like winter at night."

Jade looked outside as if she was trying to see what he saw. When he saw her smile, Ethan knew she saw it, too.

"Not much farther. Do you see those floodlights over there?" Ethan pointed across Jade's body so she would look out her window. The closeness he felt surprised him. Or, maybe it was the fact that he noticed how close they were at all.

"Yeah, I see them," Jade answered with her head so close to the cold window it started to fog.

Ethan smirked at the sight before turning his focus back on the road and making the final turn into the lumber yard.

They drove under a large wooden sign with iron lettering that read, *Brock Lumber Company. Est 1948.*

"Nineteen-forty-eight."

Ethan looked at Jade when he heard her whisper. She looked at him, then back to the sign shaking her head.

"It's nothing," she said, answering his look. "It's just a long time ago."

He drove them through the parking lot, onto a snow-covered drive that took them to the center of the yard.

"Well, here we are." Ethan put the car in park and looked around.

The floodlights were bright enough for them to see the grounds clearly. There were dark shadows where the lights couldn't reach or where there was equipment or piles of wood stacked impossibly high, but it was enough.

They saw paths through the snow that had been muddied by work boots that led to the different areas of the yard. And, from their seats in the car, they could see the wet-stained wood on the stairs that led up to an office that overlooked the grounds.

Then there were the endless stacked piles of planed woods in different sizes. And, there were piles of long tree skinny tree logs and others that had big fat trunks.

Ethan smiled at the sight. It always kind of reminded him of his truck and log playsets as a kid.

"This is amazing."

Jade's voice pulled Ethan out of his memory.

"Amazing?" He asked, turning a questioning look at Jade, who was looking around in wonder.

"Yes. Just think, your grandpa started this – though, it probably looked nothing like this – in nineteen-forty-eight. Can you believe that?" Jade's eyes were bright and curious. "All of the hard labor – and I mean *hard* labor – they probably had to do back then. Today they have machines and equipment. What did they have then? Maybe a tractor? Some type of pully system? *Maybe* if he had a lot of money, they had some

type of conveyer, but my guess is, around that time –
after the war – it was pretty slim-pickings for most."

Ethan wondered if he was seeing the woman
who wanted to become the journalist? The news
anchor? Or the one who just wanted to tell stories about
places like this one?

This Snow Queen, he would have tuned into to
watch.

After lingering too long studying Jade's face,
Ethan looked around himself. The funny thing was,
he *knew* what the lumber yard looked like back then.
And, he could show Jade. But, what struck him, was
that he hadn't ever thought of it in quite that way.

He'd never taken the time to consider that his
grandpa started the company over seventy years ago.
And that it *had* changed. It had changed multiple times.
It had grown. And with it, the town and the prosperity
in it.

Ethan heard Jade yawn and lean back in the
passenger seat chair. She looked tired, but she was still
grinning, and he could tell her wheels were still
spinning. But she – and he – needed to sleep.

He was sure she had just as long of a day as he
did. And, though they'd been cordial for a record two
hours this evening, he wouldn't bet his Christmas
presents on the rest of their days being smooth sailing.

Jade was a spitfire. A blonde, beautiful,
ambitious spitfire. Who just happened to think he was
lazy, dirty, and good-for-nothing.

Well, Ethan thought to himself as he shifted the
car into gear, *he might have to prove her wrong.*

Jade moved her head to the left, still leaning it
on the headrest, and she asked, "You're ready?"

Ethan knew she meant to head back. But he was ready for more. Maybe come Christmas, she'd even come to like him.

"Oh, yeah. I'm ready."

CHAPTER 11

Jade had tried to sleep in, but when you live a life where every day starts at four in the morning, come five o'clock, you're wide awake and staring at the ceiling.

Her eyes had long adjusted to the light, but after a bit, she reached over and turned on the little Christmas tree she'd set up the day before. The happy lights made her smile and had her cuddling back into the warm bed for a little longer to enjoy them.

After another half hour of appreciating the cute tree and then *another* half hour of staring around the room, she couldn't take it anymore. Jade looked at the light plug-in chords dangling from the corners of her bedpost and decided there was no time like the present. She'd hunt down an extension cord so she could add more lights for her enjoyment.

Jade whipped off the covers and slid on the slippers she'd brought from home. She loved the idea of a robe, but as many times as she tried to make it work, at the end of the day, she was just a sweatshirt kind of gal. So, she reached into the top drawer that now held her sweatshirts, grabbed a cute red crewneck given to her by Deni last Christmas that read *Merry and Bright*. She threw it on over her flannel pajamas and walked out.

As soon as she was in the hall, she realized she had no idea where to go.

"Well," Jade said quietly to herself. "Maybe the garage? Or, a utility closet?"

She walked down the stairs, not trying to be quiet because she had seen Ethan move to the other end of the house when they'd returned the night before, but there wasn't much noise to be made.

As she made her way down the stairs, she glided her hand along the railing. It made her think of the decorations she'd put up in her room. She usually didn't get into decorating, but something about being in the big, beautiful house and what her room had looked like this morning had her in the mood for decking the halls – every single one of them.

Jade made her way back toward the kitchen, then through the living room, and down a long hall that led to a mudroom and side entryway. If the house had a utility closet, that's where it would be.

Jade opened and closed more doors in thirty square feet than she had in her entire condo. She'd found a water closet, a pantry, and kitchen gadget storage room, a coat closet, a laundry room – which was one of at least two since she had one upstairs on her half of the floor – and a tiny room with a desk and a phone.

Jade paused, rolled out her neck, then studied the floor with her hands on her hips.

There *had* to be another room.

Jade made her way back toward the kitchen and stopped in the hallway leading back to the library and den as she passed a lone door.

"Hmm," she said to herself, eyeing the knob.

Jade reached out to check if it was locked. When it twisted side-to-side easily, she slowly pulled it open. She inched around the corner and looked down into a dark, scary-looking stretch of stairs.

Jade cringed. The dark, unknown staircase leading to who knows where was what scary-movie nightmares were made of. The kind where you yell at the TV for them to *turn on the lights!*

But, her cord could be down there. The Boogieman was probably holding it for her.

Jade inhaled, trying to gather all the courage she could, then exhaled.

"What are you doing down here?"

Jade's scream at Ethan's voice echoed throughout the floor and down the stairs. The shrill sound of it had Ethan jumping with her.

"What do you mean *what am I doing down here?*" Jade poked Ethan's chest once she was sure she was going to live to see another Christmas. "What are *you* doing down here? Don't you sleep?"

"Asks the Snow Queen who is clomping around like a Clydesdale, slamming every door in the house at five in the morning."

Jade narrowed her eyes, then they softened. "You could hear that?"

"Uh, yeah." Ethan pointed around the hall to the left, then up. Right in the direction of his bedroom directly above where she was opening and closing all of the doors.

She peeked around the corner and assessed. "Huh, it didn't even cross my mind."

Ethan rolled his eyes. "No kidding."

"Oh, come on, it's not so bad being up early."

"What are you even doing?"

Trying to appear determined, Jade stood calm and confident as she relayed the intention behind the noise. "I was – *am* – looking for an extension cord."

"Can I ask why?" Ethen wasn't sure he wanted to know.

"Yes." Jade lifted her nose. "I want to plug in the lights I've wrapped around my bedposts."

Ethan closed his eyes. Looking like if he held them shut, the whole scene might go away, and he'd find himself in his warm bed again.

He opened a single eye to check if Jade was still standing in front of him. When she plastered a smile on her face, he groaned.

"What? You're angry that you can't just sleep your life away this morning?" Jade crossed her arms and threw another proverbial lump of coal at him. "Sorry if my being here is rubbing off on you in a sort of proactive way."

Ethan said nothing. He took a step toward Jade until their bodies were almost touching.

She couldn't back up. When she tried, the open door was blocking her way.

His face was so serious and so close to hers. Jade's heart began racing unexpectedly at the surprise of the moment.

Was Ethan leaning in to kiss her? Should she kiss back? What a weird moment to show affection.

As his face moved agonizingly slowly toward hers, her lean-in was barely noticeable, but she did it.

When his arm reached beyond her and flicked the light switch at the top of the stairs, the path to the basement lit up.

Oh my gosh! Jade couldn't believe she thought Ethan was going to *kiss* her. And worse, that she was going to let him.

That's what you get for sharing the same house with an attractive man. Your body forgets what your mind knows. Then pretty soon, you're leaning in for a kiss while being trapped between a door and a hard place.

Ethan stepped back and held a hand toward the stairs. "After you."

Jade peeked over the edge and was pleasantly surprised at what she saw.

"You're surprised?" Ethan asked, not amused. At the early hour, it would take a lot for him to be entertained.

Jade looked from the stairs to Ethan. Then she pointed down. "Yeah, it's not scary at all." She was relieved.

"Excuse me?"

"What?" Jade shrugged. "It was totally dark down there. Basements are scary. And that," she nodded down, "looks great. But?"

Ethan rolled his eyes. "Yes?"

"You've been down there before?"

"Yes."

"Don't get grumpy with me. I only want to know if there are extension cords down there. If not, I won't waste our time."

Ethan blinked at Jade. Who, in a matter of minutes, had gone from sneaky, to scared, to happy, to irritatingly efficient.

Since he was too tired to banter, he pointed down the stairs. "Just go."

After twenty minutes of his life was wasted as Jade toured every nook and cranny of the finished basement before they made it to the storage and workspace, Ethan had finally made it back upstairs. Only, not to his bedroom.

Somehow, Jade had roped him into climbing on her bed to attach the lights to the cords they'd found.

In what world did he ever think he'd be hooking up a woman's Christmas lights when it wasn't even six in the morning yet. And, not just any woman, the Snow Queen.

Hmm, Ethan's mind hung on the thought of *snow.*

"Hey, did you think more about hiking to the lumber yard today?" Ethan was genuine when he turned around with the idea and balked when he saw the blank stare on Jade's face. He wondered out loud, "Can you help me read your dull expression? I'm not following."

Ethan hid a grin as he watched Jade try and not roll her eyes.

"I'm not really the *hiking* type."

"Okay," Ethan said. "What if we use the term *walking?* You city folk do that a lot, right?"

"*You city folk?*"

"Yeah, exactly. Running around from one building to the other. To high-class dinners at high-class restaurants, with high-class people." Ethan knew he was pushing buttons, but he wanted to learn more about the Snow Queen. And, he wanted to go for a hike.

"I'll have you know," Jade started while shifting into a defensive battle stance. "I learned everything I know from my grandma. She worked hard and showed me how to work hard, too. If I'm having *high-class dinners with high-class people,* it's because I've earned it. Though, I don't expect *you* to understand that type of dedication or devotion. So, I'm sorry if I'd rather *walk* somewhere with a purpose than hike around aimlessly in the snow."

With his arms held high and his hands holding a Christmas light plug next to an extension cord, Ethan froze.

For a moment, he stood in silence. To let himself and Jade stand in the wake of her words. He didn't see her shift uncomfortably behind him, but he heard her movement.

She wasn't entirely wrong. Sure, his dedication and devotion when it came to employment might have been lacking, but when it came to his love of family and friends – even his hard-nosed dad – he loved them.

Ethan heard Jade take a breath. Most likely prepping for an apology. But he didn't want one. What he wanted was fresh air.

Before Jade could speak, Ethan turned. "So, you *will* walk to the lumber yard with me? Or, was that a no?"

Through her frustration, he saw a hint of amusement.

Jade took another breath. "Fine. Yes. Let's walk."

It wasn't snowing, but that didn't mean there wasn't a foot of snow on the ground already. And yes, Jade lived in the city – and walked almost everywhere – but as she sucked freezing breaths of cold air in and out, she realized it was *definitely* not the same as walking through snow.

"You said…it wasn't…that far." Jade gasped between heaves of breath.

Her legs were burning, her face was freezing, and her body was sweating.

"It's not," Ethan said without trouble as he lifted another leg high before plopping it back into the snow before pulling out the other. "We drove here last night. You know it's not far away."

"Why does it *feel* like it's ten miles?" Jade asked, irritated at how easy it seemed for Ethan. *And,* how pleased he seemed to be that she was struggling.

Jade thought about his potential answers. "Never mind," she said finally. She just needed a break. "Hold on." Jade lifted a gloved hand, knowing Ethan couldn't see it as he was at least ten feet in front of her.

Just as she hit her knees to rest, she heard the crunching of Ethan's boots in the snow come to a stop.

"I just need a minute."

"If you're sore, you shouldn't stop for too long. Might stiffen up."

Jade looked up. "Thanks." She hoped it sounded like his advice was the last thing she wanted to hear.

"I told you, you should have had more than coffee for breakfast."

"Not helping right now." Jade heard her stomach growl at the thought of food and hoped Ethan couldn't hear it.

"Come on." Ethan trudged around her, put his gloves beneath her arms, and tugged her up in a swift, fluid motion. He started wiping off her jacket and snow pants, then removed her gloves one at a time, shaking the snow off of them, then replacing them on her hands, being careful not to get any snow on the inside.

Jade stared at him as he performed the task. He hadn't thought twice about helping her. It had come so naturally.

She squinted at him as he talked and looked off into the distance. She heard enough of the information to feel a glimmer of hope, but mostly she was vaguely intrigued by Ethan.

"Okay, remember when we were driving last night, and we took that last right before pulling into the yard?" Ethan didn't wait for her response before finishing. "That's right up there."

Jade watched him nod to an opening in the trees up ahead. She couldn't remember the last time she was so happy about anything. If she hadn't been afraid that her tears would freeze to her face, she would have cried.

"Okay, okay," Ethan said, looking Jade in the face and seeing her effervescent eyes gloss over. "That's enough. Let's just finish up. You can save your tears of joy for the day after Christmas."

Jade sniffed and looked at him. "I don't know if I've ever been so happy. Or wanted a nap so badly."

"Yeah, well, try sleeping past four AM tomorrow."

Jade sarcastically mimicked Ethan's words but couldn't stop the curve of her lip.

They hiked in silence for the next ten minutes, and like a gift from the heavens, as they crested over the last small hill, Jade saw the top of the lumber yard tower and some of the cranes they'd seen the night before.

"That old, tattered brown office is the best thing I've ever seen. I wonder if that's how all those angels and that little drummer boy felt when they saw the Christmas star?"

Ethan laughed and shook his head. "Alright, Snow Queen. Let's get you over there. I know they have a Saturday shift. Maybe they'll have a donut you can eat to save you from further delirium."

"I would give away every potential Christmas present for a donut."

Nodding, Ethan said, "I bet you would."

"Hey, down there!"

Jade and Ethan looked up to see a Paul Bunyan-sized man standing in what Jade considered the perfect lumber yard outfit. He wore a red buffalo checkered shirt, blue work jeans, and dirty black work boots. But, her favorite part was the hat with floppy ears that reminded her a little of Elmer Fudd. And under the hat was the roundest face and the most prominent brown beard she'd ever seen.

Jade heard Ethan reply. "Hey, there. It's Ethan Brock and Jade Conner. We're staying at the Brock residence. Mind if we take a bit of a tour today?"

"Oh, sure. Sully told me we'd have visitors. C'mon up."

When Jade and Ethan climbed the stairs, she learned Paul's name was Jeb Woodmaker.

"I decided, given my last name, I had to capitalize on it."

Ethan grinned, nodded, and shook Jeb's hand. "Seems like a good enough reason to work a lumber yard to me. This is Jade Conner." Ethan stepped to the side so Jade could shake Jeb's hand. "She's Helen's granddaughter."

Jeb's eyes lit up. "Really? We've heard all about you. Great to meet you. Can I offer either of you coffee or a Christmas caramel roll?"

"Yes!" Jade heard herself cheer the response. "Caramel roll, please." She looked at Ethan and repeated Jeb's words just in case Ethan hadn't heard correctly. "He said *caramel roll.*"

Then Jade tilted her head back toward Jeb. "What makes it a *Christmas* caramel roll?"

Jeb grinned and patted his belly. "Cindy adds extra caramel, pecans, and chocolate-covered toffee bits to the rolls from now straight through Christmas Eve."

Jade felt her mouthwatering. "I love Cindy. Whoever she is." She meant every word.

"I'll take that as a *yes.*" Jeb's laugh sounded like he looked – big and gruff. "Right this way."

Jeb led Jade about twelve steps into the room, where a tall wooden table was pushed up against a wall. On it sat a coffee machine, paper cups, napkins, small paper plates, and a glorious white box filled with Christmas caramel rolls.

"About ten minutes ago, I thought this might be the worst day of my life." Jade turned her big doe eyes on Jeb. "Now, I think it might be the best."

"Just wait 'til you try 'em. Help yourself. We've got all day to do whatever you'd like." Then, Jeb turned so he could see Ethan and Jade. "I've got some paperwork to get to this morning, but whatever you're interested beyond what I can show you, I'll have Kurt Cramer take you around, answer any questions. He's the one down there with the blue hat and brown jacket and pants."

"Sounds great. Thanks." Ethan stopped and covered his grin as he watched Jade take a humongous bite of caramel roll.

"Oh my *God.*" Jade saw Ethan judge either the bite, her moan of delight, or all of the above, but she didn't care. "This is the best caramel roll I've ever had. Of course, it's a Christmas caramel roll. It makes you feel like it's Christmas morning. Because something this good should be a celebration kind of thing."

"I'll let Cindy know you said so. Or, better yet. She runs the diner in town. Why don't you two come on in for coffee? A bunch of the crew head in there every morning between six and seven. We have coffee and a quick bite before starting the workday."

Jade plastered a smile on her face as she moved across the room with a giant chunk of caramel roll held out in front of her. "It sounds great. But, I don't know if Ethan will be up by then."

She waited for Ethan's scowl before lifting her hands to his face. "Try this." Jade moved so quickly that if Ethan hadn't opened his mouth, he would have had a face full of caramel and chunky bits of pecan and toffee.

Jade studied Ethan as he chewed, then beamed when his eyebrows lifted. "See? Christmas morning, right?"

"Very *Christmas morning.* I'd get up for that. Count us in. Not sure what day we'll be by, but you'll see us there."

It sounded friendly enough. But Jade wondered if Ethan's interest was genuine or if he was just checking another requirement off the list. Either way, Jade would run all the way there in the middle of a blizzard if it meant she could get her hands on more Christmas caramel rolls.

After Jade finished the roll, she and Ethan followed Jeb through a five-minute tour of the stand that easily could have been two minutes given its size. But the way Ethan was asking question after question had Jade wondering if *he* shouldn't be a journalist.

Of course, she wasn't in a hurry, and really, it just saved her from asking because she had been wondering the same things: *How many guys are on staff? How many shifts do they run? Where do they sell? What do they sell? How many trees do they use in a year? Is anything wasted? How many trees do they plant?*

Jade was pleasantly surprised by all of the answers – especially the latter. For every one they cut down, two go up. And not a single part of the tree is wasted, from branches to bark.

After a bit, they were handed off to Kurt Cramer, who spoke like he was living his dream as a lumberjack. He loved all of it, all year round. Winter was the best, though. According to Kurt, there wasn't a better thing in the world than leaving the yard at night after a hard day's work, when it was just him, the night, the snowy path, and trees lining his walk out.

Jade had to admit, the way he described it sounded ruggedly romantic. If it had been her story, she would have used words like *beautiful* or *magical*, but those words didn't do when she imagined a lumberjack walking down a snow-covered road at night. Just him, his trees, and the stars above him. It was peacefully handsome and manly.

Kurt proved to be everything Ethan had been looking for in a guide. By the time they hit hour two of the tour, Jade was wondering what else she could possibly learn about the lumber industry. And, the amazing part was, every new question Ethan asked and every answer Kurt provided interested her.

Finally, after three hours, Kurt seemed to run out of things to say. So, he offered the next best thing. "Want to try out some of the equipment?"

The way Ethan's eyes lit up reminded Jade of a kid that had just been handed a toy he'd always dreamed of.

Jade shook her head. "It's not for me. But Kurt, I think Ethan's your guy. I can wait for you up in the office."

"You're sure?" Ethan asked, even though it sounded more like, *please let me stay and play just a little bit longer.*

CHAPTER 12

Ethan knew he'd spent too long with Kurt operating the debarkers, sawmills, stackers, sorters, and conveyors. But when he looked at his watch and saw he'd been at it for four hours, he felt the panic set in. And during the minutes after, when he couldn't find Jade anywhere, the feeling turned to dread.

Ethan started his walk, anticipating the worst. When he got home, he'd probably encounter an *evil* Snow Queen for having left her alone so he could play with lumber equipment. But even then, Ethan couldn't help but feel the satisfaction from working with his hands all day long. He liked seeing the fruits of his labor. And when you started with a log that looked just as round and jagged as any old tree and put some good old-fashioned hard work into it, it turned into beautiful sheets of smooth wood.

And knowing what he'd done today would help build a house or a dining room table that family would gather around night after night made him feel pretty good.

As the sun fell behind a field of evergreen trees on the last half mile of his walk back, he also understood a little bit of what Kurt had been talking about earlier that morning. The quiet, blue-black sky, the stars lighting his way, reflecting off the snow, with a line of trees guiding him home. It was as close to perfect as he figured a moment could get.

The exact opposite of what he'd find on the other side of the front door he'd finally made it to.

Ethan stood with his hands on his hips, not ready to make his entrance. The Snow Queen was feisty and had a knack for driving home the inadequacies she thought he had. Leaving her in a square box of an office looking over a lumberyard for hours couldn't have given him a checkmark on the right side of that list.

Ethan sucked in a breath, then pulled the lever on the door handle to let himself in.

One step inside the door, Ethan was hit with the blaring sound of rock and roll Christmas tunes and the smell of…what? Ethan closed his eyes and sniffed the air.

He whispered, "Is that pizza?"

Ethan discarded his boots first, then draped his jacket over the entryway chair and tossed his hat and mittens on top before moving straight down the long hall toward the kitchen and the sound.

Not wanting to give himself away, he poked his head around the corner and saw Jade singing terribly to *Santa Claus is Comin' to Town* by Springsteen while pounding her fist into the center of a dough ball on the counter to the beat of the song.

Flour had smeared across the top of her forehead in a long streak. Then, in an unusual moment of wild imagination, he pictured himself wiping it away from her face.

Ethan shook his head to rid himself of the vision, but then his eyes moved to her blonde hair that was pulled back in a low bun, so those little wavy pieces fell out and floated in front of her face, swaying with her movements. It looked like she'd showered and dressed in an effortless sweater and jeans that looked good on her. But that was an issue. He shouldn't be noticing them at all.

But at that moment, Jade looked like what a beautiful, happy woman would want to look like in winter. Like one of those catalogs trying to sell a feeling or an image rather than their overpriced sweater.

A buzzer pulled Ethan out of his daydream. He refocused and watched Jade move to the oven. When she opened it, the scent of salty tomatoes and extra cheese billowed out. Jade easily slid a long wooden paddle beneath the pizza, pulled it out, then shook it onto a circular wooden board that was sitting next to an open bottle of wine and another pizza ready to be tossed in.

As much as Ethan could have watched her casual movements all night, the small deli sandwich he and Kurt stopped mid-day for wasn't quite cutting it. He was hungry, and his mouth was salivating.

He stepped back a couple of paces, looked around, then back a couple more. He gauged the sound of the music and the volume he'd need to use to yell down the hall. He tried once and stopped, deciding there was no way Jade heard him. He shuffled a little closer, then tried again.

"Hello! I'm home. Anybody here?" Ethan rolled his eyes at his question. Like the blaring music and the perfect smelling house didn't make the answer obvious.

"In here!" There was a pause. "In the kitchen."

The correction had him grinning. *In here*, in their grandparent's house, could have you trying four times with four misses before finding the room you were searching for. He appreciated it, even though he knew exactly where she was.

Ethan wasn't expecting what came next.

As soon as he turned the corner to the kitchen – the same one he'd been using as a hiding place only moments before – Jade walked over to him and handed him a glass of wine.

He took it, froze, and stared.

"I figure you're more of the beer type, but the wine looked good when I started smelling the pizza."

Ethan had to blink a couple of times so his eyes wouldn't start to water from holding them open. He watched Jade turn and give him a questioning look.

"Ah, I thought you'd be mad," he admitted.

Jade sipped then set her flour-dusted wineglass on the counter. "Oh, don't worry, I was. When you were going on hour two of your bromance, and I thought I was going to have to trudge back here by myself, *mad* is an extremely nice way to put it."

Ethan swallowed.

"But," Jade smiled, "Jeb was heading out to lunch, and he offered me a ride back. I took a couple of aspirin to make sure my sore muscles can move tomorrow. I took a long, hot shower. I researched some

new jobs in the city. And I talked to my sister. Deni –
my sister – is who you have to thank for my mood and
the dinner."

"Is that so?"

"It is. Apparently, the one time she saw you, she
felt you were attractive enough to warrant a pass on
today's abandonment. Then she suggested that pizza
makes everybody happy. So, I decided, since my
afternoon was actually quite nice, to come down and
make dinner."

Ethan didn't move, and he didn't say anything.
He just took everything in.

Finally, he nodded.

He thought Jade seemed satisfied that her
message of disappointment was evident. So, he said the
only thing he thought would wiggle his way back under
her skin.

"So, your sister thinks I'm cute?"

"Really?" Jade's voice sounded like her
stupefied face looked. "*That* is what you took away
from my explanation?"

Ethan shrugged. "Well, yeah. Everything else
seemed to work out pretty good." He tried to lay his
casual tone on thick.

When Jade tried to wipe a wisp of hair away
from her face, she left another smear of flour across her
cheek. Ethan pinched his lips as he waited.

"Pretty good? Pretty. Good?" Jade repeated the
question for emphasis, and Ethan decided that he liked
it.

"Let me tell you about *pretty good*. While you
were out there playing with power tools, *I* was working
on a list of employees that we should invite to the

Christmas party. And, it's all of them, by the way. Then, when I finished, I made a list of how much food we'll need for the dishes we'll need to prepare. And it's the biggest grocery list I've ever made."

"Then," she continued after a sip of wine. "I came back here, to a home that I hate that I love, to an emptiness inside of me that I'll never be able to get back. So, I showered while I cried, put on clothes that made me feel a little better, and called my sister because even though she can be a pain in the *donkey*, she always seems to know what to say when I need to hear it. And," Jade said, now flustered, "she knows I love pizza."

Jade ended with another sip of wine – only it was more like a gulp.

Ethan wondered why Helen marrying his grandpa hurt her so much. He wanted to ask, but he didn't feel he had the right. Not only after today when he'd left her alone but because they'd never been able to talk – about anything – without snarky remarks or one taking a jab at the other.

After a minute, Ethan said the only thing he could think of to say and hoped it kind of covered everything. "Jade," he waited until she looked at him. "I'm sorry."

Jade blew a breath up to try and get that stubborn blonde strand off of her face. She looked at Ethan, and as if she were too exhausted to argue, she accepted his apology and just said, "Thanks."

Sitting silently around the dinner table, enjoying what Ethan thought was the best pizza he'd ever had, he recalled Jade's day and the words she'd used to describe it.

Then he cracked.

First, a hiccup of a laugh slipped out. Then the floodgates opened. He was laughing so hard, that the only thing Jade could do was shake her head and laugh along with him.

Finally, as Ethan appeared to exhibit a hint of control, Jade asked, "What are you laughing at?"

Ethan dropped his head to compose himself, then looked her right in the eyes. "Did you really call your sister a *pain in the donkey?*"

Jade lifted her chin, but let out another little laugh. Then she shrugged. "I can't swear on TV. I find it much easier to have word replacements. And the term *donkey* is both useful and accurate."

Ethan nodded, appreciating the explanation.

"And, Ethan Brock, if you're wondering, yes, I also called you a donkey today."

CHAPTER 13

They'd made it two whole days and three whole nights together. Jade had never been so happy for a Monday in her entire life. And, now that it was officially December, it meant she only had twenty-five more days of coexisting with Ethan and twenty-six days until they could divvy up their generous earnings.

Surprisingly, having to live with Ethan wasn't as terrible as she thought it would be. The part that was affecting her more than she'd thought it would was living with the memories – both lived and lost – of her grandma.

That *and* the nagging idea of accepting money she felt like she hadn't earned didn't sit well with her. But she couldn't dwell on that. She needed to do this to ensure her carefully planned life stayed on track.

In the end, hopefully, this holiday season would be just a tiny snow-covered speedbump she needed to roll over on her way to a successful career. Soon she'd be back in the game as a news anchor with a beautiful condo that wouldn't feel so overpriced – because she'd be able to afford it.

Thankfully, Jade and Ethan had agreed to take Monday off – or at least, as much as they could. Of course, they'd still share meals, an outdoor activity, and reading in the den. But other than that, Jade was free.

Jade sat in her room for a bit in the morning after breakfast with Ethan. They'd shared small talk and, surprisingly, didn't find much to argue about. She was also shocked that he had been dressed and ready for the day.

He had been bundled up in a thick wool outdoorsman work shirt and jeans that looked like they could battle the cold weather. She figured he was off to meander around the property and wander aimlessly through the snow. When Jade learned that he was headed for the lumber yard again, she was happy she'd kept her mouth shut about him not having a purpose.

They'd finished their meal together, washed and dried their dishes, and Jade had leaned against the island as she watched Ethan walk down the long hallway toward the front door.

It all seemed so domestic. Like she had been a wife seeing her husband off for a day of work before she began a day of her own. And, there was another feeling she couldn't quite place.

Even now, as Jade laid on her bed staring up at the lights Ethan had helped her plug in, she tried to pinpoint what it was.

She remembered looking at Ethan and studying his face. The long lines where his smile had made permanent creases by his mouth, the tiny crow's feet that played at the side of his eyes, and the trimmed beard he seemed to have no intention of shaving. She had found him attractive – ruggedly so.

Somehow, in only a few days, her opinion of his appearance had shifted from unkempt to undeniably attractive.

But, Jade had to admit, though she found Ethan attractive, it didn't mean she couldn't appreciate having the house to herself.

Jade rolled off of her back to rest on her elbows. She looked around the room and saw the second box that had been left for her.

She sighed. She wasn't ready to read what was waiting for her in the letters. She didn't want the feelings or the heartbreak. She didn't want to miss the grandma she used to know more than she already did.

Or, Jade thought as she took her eyes off of the box and looked outside at the gray winter day, she wasn't ready to change her mind about Lenny Brock. Because if she was wrong about her grandma's late husband, it meant she was wrong about the betrayal she felt. And, it also meant she was wrong for removing herself from her grandma's life.

Jade closed her eyes and tried to push away the thought. She needed a distraction.

Swinging her feet over the side of the bed, she looked around.

"Hmm," she said aloud as her eyes rested on the open bedroom door. If she wasn't ready to look through the letters, maybe she could look through the house.

A devious, excited smile played across her face, and she jumped up.

"This," Jade said as she moved into the hall to look over the long catwalk that connected one side of the second floor to the other, "requires hot chocolate."

Ten minutes later, with hot, sweet-smelling chocolate wafting up to her as she walked, Jade made her way to one side of the first floor.

She wandered from room to room, baffled at how it seemed to keep going. She sipped as she poked her head into a main floor guest bedroom, then a bathroom, and then to a room that appeared to be for sewing and crafts.

Jade moved slowly and methodically. She brushed her fingertips along the wainscoting decorating the hallway walls and around framed artwork as she passed by.

When she came to yet another door, she turned a brass knob and pushed the door open. As Jade stepped in, her breath hitched.

Framed pictures of family and friends covered every inch of the walls. Jade spun in a circle to take in the enormity of the room. She stood in awe at the time and attention it must have taken to plan and place all of the photographs. And as her eyes traveled from picture to picture, she had to swallow the lump in her throat brought on by the overwhelming emotion.

As she stopped her turn, Jade moved closer to one of the walls and gasped. A picture of a little girl wearing a party dress and a crown drew her in. The girl was standing on a chair behind a birthday cake with a smile on her face that could have lit up the world.

Jade brought a hand to her mouth as tears welled in her as she looked at the picture of herself as she celebrated her third birthday.

Her hand moved to the image and touched her printed face. It had been one of the best moments of her life. She remembered the day so vividly. The moment could have been three years ago, rather than thirty.

Jade let her fingertips linger as her eyes moved to pictures of her parents, sister, aunts, uncles, and cousins. All of them captured in happy moments. There were more pictures of birthdays, summer gatherings, and Christmas parties.

She stopped once more as her eyes fell upon a picture similar to the first one she'd seen. Only this was of a young boy. He couldn't have been older than five. He was sitting on the lap of a young Lenny Brock and a woman who wasn't her grandma.

They all looked so joyful and carefree. Their eyes were wide with laughter as they posed for the camera.

The boy was undoubtedly Ethan. The hair was the same shade of brown, and the smile – though younger – held the same mischievous slanted angle.

Jade couldn't resist the bubble of laughter that escaped as she imagined what they must have been feeling at that moment.

But, even as the feeling of the image took hold, so did the woman seated next to Lenny, who must have been Ethan's grandmother.

It was then when Jade realized she wasn't the only one who had lost a grandparent. She wasn't the only one who must have felt like one of their favorite people had been left behind when Lenny and her grandma decided to marry. Ethan must have experienced the hurt just as she had.

Yet, as Jade continued around the room and saw more pictures of Ethan and Lenny throughout the room, she realized Ethan had continued his relationship with his grandfather.

Jade paused in front of a picture of a grown Ethan, with the same handsome face she knew now, sitting next to – and holding the hand of – an elderly and frail Lenny Brock.

The pang of regret was quick and unexpected.

Jade closed her eyes.

She was driven and successful. She thought she was strong. Yet, as she looked at Ethan holding his grandfather's hand, she felt a hint of jealousy of a man who she thought hadn't found a single purpose in his life.

Jade backed away from the wall, did a final turn in the room, then moved back into the hallway and closed the door behind her.

She had too many days left in her grandma's borrowed home to let thoughts of jealousy and missed opportunities haunt her. It was supposed to be a time of joy and wonder.

She inhaled and exhaled a deep breath, then turned and moved slowly to the next room.

"Hello? Is anybody home?"

Jade heard Ethan call from the front of the house.

"Hello! I'm, um, I'm–" Jade started while she looked around.

Where in the heck was she?

She poked her head out of a room on the opposite end of the house than she'd started in earlier that morning.

Her head moved back and forth as she took in her surroundings, then she yelled, "Move toward the kitchen. Then go left through the living room toward the mudroom. Follow the sound of my voice!"

Jade smiled as she heard Ethan's laugh at her directions. Then, she stood with her hands on her hips as she waited for him.

"Hey, there you are." Ethan stepped into the oversized closet and mirrored her stance. "What are you doing in here?"

Jade tried to ignore the feeling of how close Ethan was to her, but she could feel the chill from outside that lingered on his body. And she could smell the clean, fresh scent of snow.

Jade cleared her throat and tried to focus on Ethan's question.

"What do you see when you look at this room?" Jade asked, answering his question with one of her own.

Ethan looked around, taking her question seriously. He shrugged. "Jackets, snow pants, boots, shoes." He turned to look at the wall behind him. "More jackets, sweaters. Hats on the rack over there. Why?"

Jade nodded and smiled. "Want to know what I see?"

Ethan grinned, and Jade spied on it from the corner of her eye.

"Do I have a choice?" he asked.

"No, not really."

"Then let's have it."

Jade turned and took in what she'd seen before Ethan joined her in the closet. Then she stilled and stepped forward, reaching out toward two jackets. "Everything has a pair. A match."

She lifted the arms of both jackets and moved slightly to show them to Ethan. "For every winter jacket, there's a match. For every pair of snow boots, there's a match. Look," she said, moving to yet another set of hangers. Jade reached in and pulled out two pant legs. "A pair for my grandma and a pair for Lenny – your grandpa."

Ethan smiled at Jade's curiosity and the satisfaction of her discovery.

He asked, "What does this lead you to believe?" Then, quickly, he added, "Aside from the obvious point that your grandma was a more avid outdoorswoman than you?"

"Ha-ha, *very* funny." Jade faked the laugh. But she thought about what the contents meant as she dropped the snow pants and moved back into the center of the closet next to Ethan.

"I think, or, it leads me to believe, that our grandparents did everything together." Jade looked up at Ethan. "I didn't notice it until today, but this isn't the only room that's like this. In the den, there are two sets of everything – drink glasses, blankets, coasters. Even those stir sticks sitting in that silver container."

Ethan's eyebrow lifted at the observation, but Jade didn't give him more time to consider it.

"The library has two desks. One looks like your grandfather used it for the lumber yard, and another that my grandma must have used to write her letters. Then there are the other rooms. Each room seems like it's shared equally. Equal parts of my grandma and your grandpa."

Jade thought about it more. It was hard for her to admit, but she finally said, "It makes me feel like they were true companions."

Then Ethan said the words she wouldn't allow herself to think. "Or, true loves."

CHAPTER 14

The next morning brought the kind of pretty, fluttering snow that makes Christmas so magical. And Jade and Ethan were enjoying it in town at the local diner owned by Cindy. Or, as Jade was referring to her, *the Christmas Caramel Roll Queen.*

Which, Jade decided, was a much more endearing term than *Snow Queen*, which Ethan continued to call her.

The diner itself was small. There was a single row of booths near the front windows and a long line of stools that bellied up to a counter-height bar where people could sit by themselves or with friends as they enjoyed coffee, breakfast, or pie.

But, Jade and Ethan realized the size of the diner didn't matter when it came to decorating for Christmas. Every spare corner had a Christmas tree, every surface had a holiday knick-knack, and every window had garland, lights, and a spray of flocking.

The early hour was lively and festive. Jade could even hear the faint sound of Christmas music through the coffee talk of the working townspeople and the old regulars.

"I think this is my new favorite place," Jade said as she sipped her coffee and looked around. "It's so *vibrant!*"

Ethan's eyes grew with surprise. He checked out the table of old geezers next to him and wondered if they were included in Jade's description?

"What?" Jade asked at the look her comment received.

"I didn't take you for the type of woman that would get into the small-town diner scene."

"Well." Jade lifted her nose, trying not to get defensive. "I happen to enjoy many things. And, if I'm being honest with myself – and you – I'll be the first to admit I used to be a scant Christmas decorator. But, after being here, I find there's a certain appeal to this..." Jade paused to wave her hands in the air, "*chaotic* style of decorating."

"Very interesting. It seems you're having a revelation of sorts," Ethan offered.

Jade nodded dutifully. "As a matter of fact, I–"

Jade's words drifted off as she noticed one of the old TVs hanging in the corner of the room.

Ethan furrowed his eyes at her abrupt pause, then turned to see what had distracted Jade.

Jade stared at the local news channel as a bright, happy-looking woman delivered the opening line of the morning news with a smiling face, one hand on the papers in front of her and the other resting on a belly that looked like it was about ready to burst.

Jade was locked in until the view switched over to a journalist who looked like they were onsite at a local campground that offered lodging for a winter getaway. As the screen made another change, Jade looked back at Ethan.

"I'm sorry, it just caught my attention," she said.

Ethan wondered, "Anything in particular?"

Jade shook her head. "It just reminded me so much of where I started. Local, small. Doing stories just like this one." Jade motioned to the monitor that was showing a quaint, wooded cabin.

She smiled and looked back at Ethan. "I had so much fun. When I started, we were all young, trying to make something of ourselves. We'd do the show in the morning or night, then spend what we had left of our money on greasy breakfast or midnight taco runs – depending on what terrible shift we were working. Then we'd all head back to our shared city apartments or studios before doing it all over again the next day."

"What I heard from what you just said is that you don't think waking up at four in the morning is a *terrible* shift?"

Jade laughed. "Very funny. But, no. When I snagged a lead anchor position on Cities One – on the morning show no less – it was the first time I felt like I was making it."

Ethen eyed her curiously. "What happened?"

Jade knew what he was asking. *What happened?* As if she knew exactly what she did to lose the position that gave her credibility.

She shrugged. "I don't know. I'd never practiced so hard, read so much, or been so in-tune with my career and where I wanted to end up."

Jade took a sip of her coffee. She shook her head.

"I thought I was getting a promotion," she said, staring at the lights on the miniature Christmas tree that sat on their table. Then she looked up to see Ethan looking directly at her, listening intently.

Jade exhaled, then explained, "The day they let me go, I thought they were calling me into the office to give me a promotion. A spot on the evening news. The most popular, most-watched news slot of the day."

They sat together in silence for a bit before Ethan said, "I'm sorry. I don't know what that feels like, but I'm sorry."

Jade nodded. She didn't intend to be cruel, but she got lost in her sadness. "No, well, you wouldn't. Would you?"

Ethan's eyes didn't waver from hers. He just took the hit and gave a slight nod. "No. I wouldn't."

When Jade stood to put her jacket on, she noticed that Ethan didn't rise with her. She didn't blame him. But, as sorry she was for the comment, she was happy for the time alone.

She started to walk out of the diner but stopped next to the table and said, "I'm going next door to look for invitations for the Christmas party."

Ethan didn't look up, and he didn't say anything. He just lifted his coffee mug back up to his mouth to take another sip.

Jade spent the rest of the morning walking up and down the snowy sidewalk of the small town. She nodded and smiled as she passed a few familiar faces from the lumber yard, and she was stopped a couple of times by people who had met and known her grandma and Lenny Brock.

It had been unusual talking to people who had only known the two of them together. Like nobody knew about, or cared to recognize, the lives they had before they married for the second time. It was like her grandfather hadn't ever been a part of her grandma's life.

The sting of their kind words and the sympathy of her grandma and Lenny's passing touched her eyes, and she knew it was time to head back.

When she reached the house, Jade couldn't control the swell of emotion that took her over as she walked inside. Rather than fight it, she let the sadness take over. She ran up the stairs to her bedroom and didn't stop until she slammed the door behind her.

Jade fell against the back for the door and let all of the tears fall that she'd been holding in and ignoring for years. She spun and screamed, then moved to the box of letters she'd set on her borrowed dresser and pushed them to the floor.

As the letters scattered around the room, Jade stilled. She wiped her eyes, turned, crawled into bed, and pulled the covers over her head.

Three hours had passed since Ethan stood outside the car and watched Jade run into the house ahead of him. He wondered what had happened in town that had caused such a shift in her. One moment they were coexisting nicely. He would have even considered the two of them friendly. Then another she was running away.

It couldn't have been just about the job. There was more.

Ethan sat in the den with a whiskey to warm him and a Christmas puzzle to keep him busy.

It allowed his mind to wander and wonder. He didn't *want* his head to do either of those things because his mind wouldn't stay off Jade.

She had been angry when she said the hurtful words to him at the diner. But, as painfully straightforward as they were, weren't they also true?

He didn't know what it was like to want something that badly. Then to get so close, just to have it taken away from you.

From the work angle, he had nothing to offer Jade. He didn't know what she was going through. She hadn't shared with him the sudden change in her mood. She *definitely* didn't seem like she wanted to share why she'd gotten so emotional all of a sudden. But there were things he could do.

Ethan absently played with the corner puzzle pieces he'd separated from the rest and thought about what they needed to do. They needed to eat. They needed to do an activity. And they needed to decorate.

Those were all things he could do to help.

Ethan eyed the puzzle, found an edge piece that fit together with the border he'd created, and shoved back from the table.

Ethan rolled his neck and shoulders, threw back the last of his whiskey, and marched with a new sense of determination toward the kitchen.

Usually, he found kitchens a bit intimidating when there was another person involved. But really, the kitchen was just another room with things plugged into walls that he used when he was feeding himself. He could navigate it, throw something together, and if it tasted terrible, he could end the night with frozen pizza, and nobody would be the wiser.

But, when another person depended on your ability not to burn down the house, that was a completely different story.

Ethan rocked back and forth in front of the fridge. He pulled drawers open, took inventory of what was hidden behind condiments, and studied the contents of the door shelves.

All in all, dinner looked promising. Ethan found cheese, bread, and butter – all staples in a proven comfort food staple.

He sidestepped to the panty and flung the door open, hoping for the best.

And, there it was – a glorious can of tomato soup.

Ethan threw his hands in the air and sent a silent *hooray* to the winter food gods because tonight, they would eat!

He pulled everything out, set it on the counter, then checked his watch. There was a good half hour before he'd need to come back in to start making dinner. It was just enough time to get started on the rest of his plan.

Ethan worked outside first since he'd lose good working light quickly with the sun going down before dinner. So, he hauled a wheelbarrow to the back of the house where he'd found some dried wood, then loaded it up, and pushed it around the house, and left it for later.

"So far, so good," Ethan said, through the kind of heavy breaths only hard work could provide.

Next, he flipped on the light to the basement. He grinned a bit at the memory of Jade not wanting to go down the stairs for the simple fact that it was dark and "a basement." Apparently, it was a scary combination.

He made his way down and found the storage space. Then he looked down what seemed to be an entire wall of bins labeled *Christmas Decorations*.

"Here goes nothin'." Ethan sucked in a breath, walked to the end, and pulled the first bin off the shelf.

Thankfully, the bins had labels that told him what rooms they belonged in. But by the time he'd brought one bin of decorations to the kitchen, two to the den and library, and three to the living room, Ethan wondered if he'd be able to get up from the floor where he dropped after setting the latest bin next to him.

"So tired." Ethan breathed heavily while wiping the sweat off of his forehead with the sleeve of his flannel shirt.

He lifted his other hand and opened his eyes to view the time, then let it fall when he saw that it had taken him almost an hour to set up outside and drag only half of the boxes up the stairs.

"What are you doing?"

Ethan lifted his head off the floor to see Jade hovering over him. He laughed out of exhaustion and dropped his head back down.

"Isn't it obvious? I'm making us dinner."

He lifted his head again as Jade rewarded him with a tentative smile. He mirrored Jade's grin, then held his arms up in the air.

"What?" Jade asked. "What is that?" She pointed to his outstretched arms.

"C'mon. Just come over here. Help me up."

Jade let an unguarded laugh escape. "No way, I can't lift you."

Ethen wiggled his arms around then ended by coercing Jade closer with a wave of his hands. "Sure, you can. Help a guy up. Just give me your hands."

He waved his fingers once more and looked up to see Jade rolling her eyes. That's when he knew he had her.

Jade reached out her arms and linked her hands with his. She grunted and laughed as she tried to pull Ethan up.

"I can't!" she said, breathless from the laughter.

"You can! Pull!"

Jade heaved once more while Ethen rocked his body to give her a bit of momentum.

It sent her flying backward. Ethan gripped her hands to steady her just as she started to squeal her way to the ground.

With their hands still linked, it took them both a moment to catch their breath and stop laughing.

"Thanks," Ethan said as he bent to get a better look at Jade's face.

He could tell she'd slept, and that was good. But, he could also see that she'd been crying. Maybe he wouldn't get to it tonight, but he was going to find out why before Christmas. For now, he had a different plan.

Ethan looked at Jade. "You ready?"

"For what?" She asked.

Ethan took a chance by keeping Jade's hands in his and leading her out of the room.

"Didn't you hear me earlier? I'm making dinner."

CHAPTER 15

"Mmm, this is surprisingly delicious. Thank you." Jade dipped an end of her grilled cheese sandwich into her bowl of tomato soup and took a bite. "I thought you said you didn't have any prowess in the kitchen. What other gourmet surprises do you have up your sleeve?"

Jade tried to be friendly, but she could tell the humor hadn't yet come back from the morning they'd had in town. Nevertheless, she was trying.

"Well," Ethan started. "The possibilities are endless. They offer so many different kinds of canned soup. I can almost feed myself for an entire year. Tomato, Chicken Noodle, Butternut Squash, Split Pea. Then there're the sandwiches. Wheat bread or white, ham or turkey or salami, provolone or swiss."

"It's all awe-inspiring." This time, Jade didn't have to force her smile.

Ethan crunched through a golden edge of his sandwich and winked. "Honey, you ain't seen nothing yet. When I get fancy, I open a can of chili, top it with cheese, and sprinkle some Fritos on top."

Jade laughed and shook her head as she wondered how simple it must be for Ethan to live. Then, she thought about the meal Ethan had just described and said, "That actually sounds pretty good." Jade's words surprised even herself.

Ethan raised an eyebrow at the unexpected comment. He wasn't ready for Jade to agree with him. In fact, he'd prepared himself for another demeaning blow to his ego.

"Okay, then," he said while nodding happily. "Then count me in for chili night."

Jade held his gaze, grinned, and nodded back.

They ate in silence for a few more minutes, risking casual glances at each other. Every once in a while, their stares would hold for a moment, then one or the other would look away.

When Jade turned away the last time, her eyes fell on a box that looked similar to the ones Ethan was lying next to in the living room.

"What is that?" she asked as she finished her sandwich and leaned away from that table.

"That," Ethan said, "is Christmas."

"Christmas?" she asked.

"Yes. We, according to our list, are required to deck the halls. So that, and the others scattered around the house, are what we will deck with."

"You brought up the Christmas decorations?" Jade tilted her head and grinned.

"Well, yeah." Ethan tried to brush it off. "I wanted to help. Every now and then – even the perfect ones – need a little help."

Jade felt the blush burn her cheeks. It was sweet – *he* was sweet. At least he was for the moment. And after the way she'd treated him that morning, she didn't deserve his kindness.

"I'm sorry," Jade said the words like if she didn't say them now, she'd never get them out.

"For what?" Ethan asked as if he had no idea why she was apologizing.

Jade looked down and thought of all of the times she'd given Ethan a hard time, especially that morning at the diner.

She looked Ethan in the eye and said, "I have no right to judge the way you live your life. I was upset today, and I took it out on you. So, I'm sorry."

"Thanks," Ethan accepted Jade's apology that he didn't feel was needed. Still, he wondered, if he pressed, would the tender moment allow her to share more?

"The job isn't all that's on your mind, is it?" Ethan asked. "What happened before we drove back home today?"

Jade sighed. She was tired, but she would have talked. He'd caught her at a vulnerable moment. But, she was also confused. She didn't know how to explain what she was feeling.

"Not tonight," she said finally. "Not never," she admitted. "Just not tonight."

Ethan accepted her response, gave a single nod, and said, "Okay."

"Okay."

Jade studied Ethan as he scooped every last drop of his tomato soup out of his bowl with his spoon. She watched him lick it clean as she held her lips together to keep from smiling. Then he wiped his face with the napkins he'd set out for them.

When Ethan leaned back, he beamed. "Okay, so are you ready to do the dishes?"

The surprise at the blunt expectation had Jade laughing. "You make dinner, so now I'm on dish duty? Is that how this works?"

Ethan blinked like he wasn't following. Then it clicked. "Oh, ah, no. Since I have to go set up outside, I just thought you might want to stay inside for that. I unloaded the dishwasher. All you'd have to do is toss them in. But I can do it later."

"Sorry, what are you setting up for outside? I'm not following." Jade was confused.

"Our activity. We haven't done our outdoor activity yet today, so I got it ready before dinner. I could go finish, then come get you when it's ready."

"You...what?" Jade didn't know where to start. Ethan had spent his evening planning to take care of hers. "Thank you." She just settled on what she wanted to say. And *thank you* was it.

"Of course." Ethan shrugged like it wasn't a big deal at all. "So, I'll just come to get you in a bit then?"

"Yeah, sounds great. Do I need to get anything ready?"

"It's cold out there. Might want to throw on a hat."

Jade nodded, then watched as Ethan left her sitting at the kitchen table.

Fifteen minutes later, Jade had the kitchen spotless, and she'd dressed in her grandma's outdoor gear she'd found the day before. There was no use suffering in the cold in her adorably mediocre jacket when her grandma's light blue pillow of a jacket would keep her toasty and warm.

Jade glanced longingly at her pretty red wool dress coat, then flicked off the light and left it behind.

Just as she made her way back to the front door, Ethan opened it. His eyes immediately started to dance.

"Lookin' good."

Jade did a little spin and ended with a curtsy. "Why, thank you, I found it myself. Top of the line, old-lady's-wear. Circa nineteen ninety-nine."

"It's a classic, alright." Ethan clapped at her dance, then asked, "Ready?"

"Let's get this activity over with." Jade wasn't afraid to show her true colors. The idea of hiking through the woods or snowshoeing across the vast snowscape probably sounded terrible to most people, especially when it meant leaving the comfortable warmth of your home at seven o'clock at night for black skies and fifteen-degree weather.

Ethan held out his gloved hand. "I think you might be pleasantly surprised."

Jade placed her big mitten in his and said, "I'll be the judge of that."

Ethan pulled Jade out into the cold by the hand. He knew she was expecting something less than enjoyable by her standards. She probably thought he was going to haul her up a hill for nighttime sledding or strap some skis to the bottom of her feet and let her fly.

He grinned at the thought but decided he'd place those activities on the back burner and save them for another day.

They walked along a narrow path through an opening in the pine trees at the edge of the yard.

Ethan waited until the glow came into view and became hopeful for Jade's reaction. Then she saw it. A quick inhale at the flicker in the distance was the first sign that he'd made the right decision.

"Is that a bonfire?" Jade asked the excited question before giving Ethan a playful hit on his shoulder.

"It might be." Satisfied, Ethan placed his hand on the shoulder Jade had touched, then he watched Jade clumsily run down the shoveled path the rest of the way.

Jade slipped once and caught her balance. Then on the very next step, she hit a soft patch of snow and tumbled down.

"Oh no," Ethan mumbled to himself, hoping his idea wouldn't get ruined – especially when he heard the sound coming from ahead of him.

He quickened his pace but quickly realized Jade wasn't crying. She was laughing.

Ethan caught up and rolled Jade over onto her back. Then, with two boots straddling her body, Ethan crouched a bit to get a closer look. Jade's eyes were closed as her mitted hands covered the puffy coat over her stomach, and her laughs were so reckless and so true, Ethan wondered if he'd ever seen anything more beautiful. Jade's face glittered with snow, and frozen clumps had stuck to her hair. She was a different kind of Snow Queen entirely. Fantastic and stunning.

When Jade opened her eyes, a quick tear of laughter trickled out and caught the light of the fire.

Ethan pulled off his glove and wiped it away. The action seemed to help Jade gather herself.

Rather than let either of them linger on the tender moment, Ethan put his glove back and rested his hands on his knees.

"You're okay?" he asked.

Jade's sudden seriousness fell away, and she smiled. "Yeah. Better than."

"Good," Ethan said. "Now, how do you feel about s'mores?" He held out his hands to help her up.

"Right up there with a few of my favorite things," Jade admitted.

Ethan pulled Jade up and nodded. "Then I hope this setup will do."

They stepped forward into the opening as the dazzling flames came into full view. The fire danced and flickered, giving the snow-covered ground an enchanting sparkle. Two long logs were placed near the fire, and thick wool blankets were folded and set on each end. On the ground, there was a tray with a big thermos, an unopened box of graham crackers, two chocolate bars, and an open bag of marshmallows.

"Hmm, looks like somebody got a little hungry out here." Jade eyed the bag, then glanced at Ethan.

Ethan looked around. "And I specifically told those Arctic Puffins to stay away. Rascals."

"Arctic Puffins, you say?"

Ethan forced a guilty grin. "I still have marshmallow dust on my face, don't I?"

Jade laughed and moved closer to the fire, and Ethan followed. When she sat, he did the same. Then he offered to start roasting a marshmallow for her.

"Are you kidding?" Jade asked, holding out her hand for the roasting sticks he'd set out for them. "Roasting a marshmallow is sacred. There's only one way to do it right."

"Very interesting," Ethan said while handing Jade a roaster. Then he admitted, "I have a bad feeling about what you're about to do. Can I prep your graham and chocolate? Or, is that off-limits, too?"

"Yes." Jade was all business. "You may help with that."

Ethan tried to hold in his grin as he broke the graham in half and placed a piece of chocolate on one of the halves.

Then he watched the worst thing he'd ever seen in his life. His jaw fell open as Jade stuck her marshmallow directly into the fire.

It immediately went up in flames.

"What are you doing?" Ethan's question carried an appropriate amount of shock and playful disgust.

"I," Jade started, already defending her actions, "am creating the perfect smoky crunch on the outside of my mallow."

"You're killing it."

"I'm doing no such thing!" Jade said as she pulled her stick out of the flames to hold up what looked like a lump of coal.

Ethan pointed to it. "That is what death looks like."

"Graham now, accuse later." Jade quickly blew out the flames, then carefully placed the crispy marshmallow on the chocolate as Ethan pinched it with the top graham. She set her roaster down, then squished the two ends together and waited for the light crunch.

Ethan stared as Jade took her first bite and saw how she closed her eyes while the burnt edges of mallow mixed with the melted chocolate.

Finally, he shook his head. "I will never understand."

"There's nothing to understand. The flavor is smoky and delicious. "I suppose you're one of those who finds the perfect spot, then waits ten minutes as you try to achieve the ideal golden brown color?"

"Well," Ethan began, "at least I know I'm not the only one who's tried to have this conversation with you before, but...yes. I happen to enjoy taking the time to make sure the entire marshmallow can get soft, melty, and chewy."

Ethan nodded to Jade's hands as she brought them to her mouth to take another bite of s'more. "I can't even believe that sorry excuse for a roast melted your chocolate."

Jade's lip twitched at their banter.

Rather than argue, she finished her s'more in satisfied silence and waited for the next ten minutes while Ethan hovered over the fire, kneeling on one knee as he tried to hold his marshmallow in the perfect location.

Ethan felt her watching him. He didn't want to interrupt the thoughts that might be floating around in her mind, so he didn't risk a glance. Instead, he lingered over his s'more and enjoyed the moment. But he wished he knew how she felt, what she was thinking.

Was she enjoying this? Or was it just better than hiking a mile through the snow?

Ethan liked to think it was the former.

As he finished and licked his fingers, he didn't have to wonder anymore.

"This night – this fire – is perfect."

It sounded like she was searching for the right words to use.

Ethan looked over to her as she stared at the fire, then as she moved her eyes around to the trees that were blocking the winter wind, and finally up to take in the clear starry night. It was then when she closed her eyes and breathed deeply.

When Jade's eyes opened, she turned them toward Ethan. "This moment," she said, "*feels* like Christmas."

She shook her head and looked away as if searching for the right way to describe how she was feeling. "It feels peaceful and pretty. I should be cold from the freezing weather, the snow, and the wind, but I'm warm thanks to this hideous jacket and this exquisite, beautifully warm fire. The air smells like fresh snow, but the fire smells like crackled, fragrant wood. And every once in a while, as the wind shifts, I get just a hint of pine."

Jade inhaled as if she was trying to pull in all of the senses she had just described. "It's like Christmas in a single moment. It's wonderful." She looked at Ethan. "I love it. Thank you."

Ethan smiled and nodded. He let Jade have her moment for a good five seconds. Then he thought enough time had passed before he could try and ruin it.

"Yeah," he started. "It's okay, I guess."

"Just okay?" Jade laughed.

"Sure, it's all *enchanting* and *magical*, but what's Christmas without the tree and the lights? I haven't cursed a single strand of tangled twinkle lights, and it's already December."

"What, Mr. Brock, are you trying to say?"

Ethan slapped his knees like he thought a grumpy old man might do. "What I'm saying is, those Christmas lights inside aren't going to hang themselves. We've got decorations to place. We've got trains to set up. And dang it, we've got eggnog to drink."

Jade withheld her laughter until Ethan's mentioned the eggnog.

"Okay, okay," she said. "If you're going to ruin my moment by getting all Scrooge-y on me, I guess you leave me no choice."

Ethan watched Jade push up from the log then march away wearing big, ugly winter boots in the same baby-blue color as her jacket.

Three and a half hours later, Jade and Ethan were stretched out on the den floor next to the fire. The record player had stopped playing the last side of a Bing Crosby vinyl, and the empty sound crackled through the flaring horn as it spun.

They'd started with the kitchen and living room. They'd dug through the boxes and scattered the contents around the room. They'd placed a line of nutcrackers on the mantel, carefully set the hand-carved Santa Claus collection on the side tables, and filled a large wooden bowl with green and silver bulbs, then showed it off in the middle of the coffee table.

There were endless knick-knacks, framed Christmas pictures from holidays gone by, and Christmas books that they found special places for throughout the room. And in each box, there were homemade ornaments that they'd set aside for later.

After the living, Jade and Ethan moved into the kitchen and emptied that box as well. They'd replaced the everyday dinnerware and glasses with Christmas dishes that had images of red robins, berries, and winter twigs and branches embossed on each one. They'd moved a mishmash of mugs with reindeer, snowmen, snowflakes, and a few shaped like Santa and Mrs. Claus into the cupboard above the coffee maker. And they'd even taken the time to carefully unwrap a cookie jar that looked like an elf shoe and placed it on the counter by the stove.

Every now and then, they'd tell a story about an ornament they recognized, or they paused to refill their reindeer glasses with eggnog.

By the time they'd made it to the library and the den, the more sophisticated decorations had been a welcome change.

Where the kitchen and living room decorations had been lively, colorful, and fun, the library and den decorations were classy and sophisticated.

Going with the mood, they'd turned on the old phonograph and filed through the old records for some old Bing Crosby and Rosemary Clooney. Then, to the sound of big band Christmas tunes, they'd strung garland that looked like fresh pine on bookshelves and banisters, and placed pretty snow globes on desks and bar tops.

There were boxes with ornaments left alone for later, but all others were finished – including one with an electric train that chugged in a circle on the den floor.

When Ethan flipped the switch to turn off the train they'd watched move around the track a couple of times, both he and Jade fell to their backs in front of the fire.

Now, as they both were barely able to stay awake, Ethan nudged Jade. "We still need a Christmas tree." He turned his head to take in her profile.

Jade's eyes were closed, but her face looked satisfied.

Without moving, Jade said, "I think we need three."

"Three Christmas trees?" Ethan asked with a bit of tired laughter.

Jade turned her head, so their faces were nose-to-nose. She thought about Ethan's question and said, "You're right. We need four. Unless," Jade continued as her thoughts moved with her words, "you want one for your bedroom, too."

Ethan nodded first and watched as Jade moved her head forward again as her eyes fluttered closed.

He quickly checked his watch and saw the late hour. "It's midnight," Ethan said. "But, if you stick with me, I can find you a tree – or four."

Jade's lips turned up, and Ethan found his own doing the same.

It was quiet for a moment, so when Ethan started rustling around and reaching his hand toward the coffee table, Jade asked what he was doing.

"We still have to read."

Jade groaned. "Do we have to?"

Ethan plopped back to the floor with *A Christmas Carol* in hand and said, "I will not have every Christmas I celebrate haunted by my late grandfather for not following orders. I'll read. You listen."

Jade's agreement was barely audible.

By the time Ethan had read through a single page, he had heard the heavy breaths from Jade, falling fast asleep next to him.

He quietly closed the book, deciding that one page was good enough, then pulled a blanket off the couch and draped it over their bodies.

He gently lifted Jade's head to place it on a pillow he'd pulled down from the couch, then he grabbed one for himself.

Ethan didn't know when he finally fell asleep, but when he did, it was to the crackling and popping of the fire as he took in the pretty profile of a woman who was constantly surprising him.

CHAPTER 16

Jade hardly had time to argue with the activity Ethan had planned for them, especially since she had woken up with her head resting on his shoulder and a blanket draped over both of their bodies.

Of course, the carefree, handsome outdoorsman thought nothing of it. He had been lying there awake when she stirred out of her sleep with a sore bum and Ethan's body keeping her warm.

Good morning, how did you sleep? I didn't want to wake you.

Those were his words. He has said them as if waking up next to somebody you'd spent the last fifteen years of your life judging wasn't the most conflicting thing in the world.

And it *was* conflicting.

At the memory of the morning, Jade's eyeballs bugged out as she stared at the ski boots Ethan had found for her. Apparently, the basement was more than just Christmas Decoration Storage Central. It also stashed an endless supply of scary winter activity gear – like skis.

"You look great. Are you ready?"

Jade leaned back and looked up at Ethan. "Do you think you're going to get sick of asking me that by the time our holiday together comes to an end?"

It was a question worth asking.

Are you ready to hike? Are you ready to decorate? Are you ready to eat s'mores at this perfect Christmas bonfire?

Ethan shook his head. "Not as long as you're willing to keep hearing it."

Jade grinned and nodded. "Okay, then I guess I am."

When she stepped outside, Jade looked at the vast snow-covered land and wondered if it had ever seemed so endless.

"Don't worry," Ethan said, reading her body language that must have been screaming that it was terrified.

Jade heard his reassurance. And, surprisingly, she felt herself relax. Was this exciting for her? No, absolutely not. But was she worried?

Jade studied Ethan's profile and took in his confident, calm stance.

No, she wasn't worried.

"I'm not," Jade said finally. "As long as you're with me, I think I'll be okay."

She didn't think her words were of any considerable significance, but with the way Ethan turned to look at her, she might as well have told him he was getting exactly what he asked for for Christmas.

"Yeah," Ethan said as he blinked. "I'm with you. We're in this together."

Jade took more comfort in Ethan's words than she wanted to admit. So, to save herself from the moment, she asked, "Well, then, how do I use these things?"

Ethan started laughing as Jade began taking giant, high-knee steps to move forward. With each step, her ski came two feet off the ground, then slapped down on the snow in front of her.

"What?" Jade asked, irritated at the difficulty she was having moving forward.

"Have you *ever* seen anybody ski?" Ethan asked through freezing tears.

"Does the Olympics count?"

Ethan pointed to Jade's ski as it hovered feet above the ground. "And *that's* your interpretation of what you saw?"

Jade looked down and couldn't help the bubble of laughter at the sight of her body as it leaned to lift her foot and move it forward. "I don't know!" she laughed. "It's just what felt right!"

When Jade's ski found the snow again, it crossed with the ski she was standing on. As she tried to move the trapped ski, she lost her balance and crashed sideways into the snow.

With her feet tangled, her hand trapped in the ski pole that was, and half of her face covered with snow, Jade started laughing hysterically.

When she heard Ethan join in, she yelled through her humor and said, "Hey! Don't laugh. Help me up. I'm stuck!"

"Ha! Hold on, I'm coming."

Jade heard the same snap from Ethan's boots that she'd heard when she popped hers into the skis when they started. Then, with her body still sideways, Jade saw one of Ethan's boots stomp in front of her face and heard another crunch behind her.

"Okay. Up on three. One, two..." Jade listened to Ethan's grunt as he said the last number. "Three!"

In a single, fluid motion, Jade was on her feet.

As if it was the most normal thing in the world, Ethan's hands found Jade's jacket and pants and started brushing the snow away from them. Then, when he finished with her clothing, Ethan removed a glove and brought his warm hand to Jade's face and hair to gently push away the snow that had stuck there.

Ethan leaned back and gave her a quick once-over. When he nodded, he moved his eyes back up to Jade's. "Want to try it again?" he asked.

Jade thought about it. This was her *out*. If she wanted to, she could say *no,* then turn around and walk right back into the house. But, something about the fresh air, the tenderness Ethan was showing, and the moment they were sharing had her staying.

"I do," she said after a moment. If Ethan could do this, she could too.

At that moment, she'd had enough of letting him take care of her. She'd had enough of letting him plan their days and their activities. She could participate in this moment as much as he could.

So, it was decided. Jade nodded in agreement with her thoughts and words. "Teach me how to ski."

It didn't take long for Ethan to have Jade slowly gliding along on top of the snow. She wasn't skilled, and she didn't know if skiing would become her go-to winter sport. As far as she was concerned, roasting marshmallows over a bonfire was where she excelled, but she was hanging in there!

They hadn't gone far, and that too was nice. But, Jade realized as they slid their way across the snow, Ethan had an ulterior motive.

A long line of evergreen trees came into view as they crested over a low hill, and Jade heard the excitement in Ethan's voice. "Do you see the trees?"

"I do," Jade responded, trying to hide her skepticism.

"Perfect. That's where we're headed. We have a little job to do. Then we'll head back."

Jade squinted beneath her stocking cap as she watched the trees slowly grow taller the closer they got.

"Okay, what are we doing here?" Jade asked as she let her skis and body weight do the work to stop her movement. She unhooked one boot and then the other. Then, with her feet safely back on the ground, she threw her ski poles to the side and fell backward to sit and rest as she waited for Ethan to lay it on her.

Ethan removed his skis, pulled his gloves off, and tossed them to the ground. Then he reached into his pocket and pulled out long red ribbons. He turned and gestured his hands toward the pretty forest of trees and said, "I think you'll be able to find *at least* four magnificent Christmas trees in here."

Jade's eyes ballooned when she realized what Ethan was telling her. She wanted the house decked out with giant, pretty Christmas trees, and now was her chance to handpick the perfect ones.

Not only that, but Jade was so happy she wasn't being thrown into another miserable outdoor activity that she wasn't ready for that she leaped at Ethan and threw her arms around him.

She held for a moment and mumbled words into the front of his jacket. "I'm so happy we don't have to ski through these trees."

Ethan laughed at her muffled words and draped his arms around her for a brief moment before he patted her back.

When Jade didn't move, he suggested, "How about we hunt for the perfect tree?"

Jade pushed back, snatched a ribbon, and corrected, "Trees."

Ethan didn't know if it was the idea of lunch or the fact that the next time they headed out to the patch of trees, they'd get to use a truck, but whatever it was had Jade skiing home ahead of him the entire way.

He had to admit, he was impressed. The Snow Queen wasn't half bad after she got the hang of it.

Watching her skis cross and seeing her get tripped up on the first couple of tries – all while laughing so hard she could barely bring herself upright again – had been comical. But as sure as the snow was white, she came around. What Ethan wasn't so sure about was the twinge he got in his stomach as he wiped the snow away from Jade's face and brushed it out of her blonde hair.

That was new territory for him. He'd thought of her as pretty before. But too polished for his liking. At that moment, though, just as she had looked when she'd fallen asleep next to him, she looked natural and beautiful. Her looks, in combination with her unhindered laugh, were intoxicating. The way her head fell back and her eyes closed as the joy took hold of her body. He wasn't sure he'd ever seen anything like it.

Of course, he could never tell her that, seeing as she was merely surviving just being in the same house as he was. And she'd probably get a really good laugh if he confided any type of feelings for her.

Yeah. All these feelings were something he would have to ignore if *he* wanted to survive until Christmas.

Ethan finished frying up a second specialty of his: grilled peanut butter and jelly sandwiches. Like a grilled cheese, but sweet and salty. He slid them out of the cast iron pan and onto a couple of plates just as Jade walked back into the kitchen.

He noticed she had braided her hair and a new knit hat replaced her grandmother's old one that she'd been wearing that morning.

"It smells like I'm going to enjoy this," Jade said as she leaned over the island to spy on Ethan's culinary prowess.

"It's another staple," Ethan admitted.

"Well, let's eat so we can go chop down some trees!"

Ethan handed Jade her plate and watched her take the first gooey bite.

"You're sure you want five?" he asked again, having asked the question repeatedly while they were tree shopping through the woods that morning. She reassured him that's what she wanted every time as they were circling, studying, and smelling for the perfect trees.

"You definitely need a tree in your room. Uh-ah!" Jade lifted a finger just as Ethan started to protest. "It's only fair." Then she softened. "And, it's *such* a cute little tree."

Ethan didn't stop the playful roll of his eyes. In fact, he added to it with an exaggerated sigh and said, "If you insist. But you're helping decorate it."

Jade radiated her satisfaction and smiled. "Deal."

CHAPTER 17

Jade wondered how they could have shared such a wonderful day of skiing, dining together, picking out Christmas trees, and ended the night with a nice drink and *A Christmas Carol,* only to have the next day go so terribly wrong.

And, more importantly, why did she care?

One moment they were decorating Ethan's cute little evergreen tree in his room, and the next, they were arguing about how they both came to agree to their grandparents' absurd will requirements.

Jade had asked Ethan what caused him to say *yes.* What had made him pack up his life of luxury and move in with Jade – who was basically a stranger.

Even now, as she looked back on the argument, she probably shouldn't have agreed with Ethan's parents. But she thought it was good that they finally cut Ethan off. She thought they did the right thing by encouraging him – though Ethan didn't see it that way – to start living a life he could make all his own.

How are we any different from each other?

Ethan's question rang in Jade's mind as she slowly dressed the Christmas tree that they'd both set up in her room earlier – by herself.

Then, rather than wait for her response, Ethan had answered for her.

He had called her a hypocrite. He said that she claimed she was there to stay on track with her life's plan, but really, she was just borrowing a sorry excuse for a sob story until she could get her hands on her grandma's money. Who – by the way – Jade had decided to estrange herself from.

Rather than listen to Ethan, the mood and the moment had caused her to fight back and to argue.

He had stood his ground, and she walked out. But all it really had done was call both of them out on truths neither was willing to admit.

Now, as Jade hung another bulb next to one of the hundreds of white lights she'd wrapped around the tree, she realized she had a lot more to admit to than just biding her time until she could collect money.

It was never about the money. In fact, a little piece of her always knew she was living outside of her means. Jade loved the condo, but it felt forced. She loved the job, but it had become more about presentation than about the story. And she missed that.

Then there was her grandma. It had been hard to decide to come here because she missed her grandma, and there was still a part of her that was mad. But there was also a piece of Jade that knew she'd been wrong to remove herself from her grandma's life altogether. And *that* was hard to swallow.

Finally, there was Ethan. Jade stepped back from the Christmas tree and stepped back until she found the bench at the end of her bed. She sat and stared at the glow of the lights. It was so pretty. It was no wonder why the night decided to come early in winter. Jade decided it was something that just had to be so people could enjoy the beauty of Christmas lights just a bit longer during the holiday season.

And, as she looked on at her pretty tree, she wished Ethan was there to enjoy it with her.

That was the most surprising feeling of them all.

Jade hadn't meant to be cruel when she and Ethan got into their argument. She had tried to sound light and positive. Then offer that perhaps that his parents deciding to sell their cabin was a good thing. That maybe, being there at the house – with her – was a good thing. But it didn't come out that way.

The truth was, Jade had wanted Ethan to admit that he was happy there. That he liked their adventures together – even though she was decidedly not very good at being an outdoorswoman. But she was trying.

She wanted him to say something sweet so that she could return the gesture. And if that wasn't the biggest shock of them all, Jade didn't know what was.

But instead of all of that, she was in her room, decorating a tree alone with her thoughts. She knew eventually she'd have to leave her bedroom. She'd have to suck it up, walk out the door, and down to the den where Ethan would continue reading *A Christmas Carol.*

She wouldn't be surprised if he skipped that evening. There wouldn't be an ounce of blame she would point at him. She knew she'd hurt his feelings.

Why was it so hard to face somebody you knew you had hurt? Why did she care?

But that was just it. She did care. She cared for Ethan. And that's why it would be so difficult.

Jade sighed and stood. Before she made any decisions about the night, she wanted a warm shower. She'd take care to wash and dry her hair. She'd dress in her winter flannel pajamas for comfort. And after taking the time to sit with everything she admitted to herself that evening, she'd choose to go to the den or decide to stay in the safety of her room, where her feelings could remain intact.

Before moving to the bathroom, Jade walked to the dresser where the box of letters sat that she'd yet to read. She carefully picked it up and placed it beneath her tree. She'd have to save that for yet another day.

Ethan was a lot of things: distracted, misaligned, a disappointment. But he wasn't a coward, and he didn't back down. And, he wasn't lazy.

He might not have a job, but he was active and adventurous – and both of those things were still hard work. They just happened not to be the type of work that paid handsomely or that his dad approved of.

But he was raised to be a good man. And he had agreed to the terms of the will. And by showing up, he was equally responsible for the outcome.

So as the arm on his wall clock clicked and pointed at the seven, he pushed up from his bed and didn't think twice about making his way to the den.

It wouldn't be easy to face Jade after their exchange earlier that evening, but he was good at having hard conversations. He had years of practice with his dad. And no matter what, he showed up.

In the den, Ethan's movements had become routine. First, he either started the phonograph or flicked on the radio to fill the background with the quiet, happy sound of Christmas. Then he moved to the fireplace to start a fire with wood that he'd been dutiful in bringing inside for their use. And finally, before settling down with the book, he'd head to the bar and pour two glasses of whatever he was having.

It hadn't taken long for Ethan to realize Jade didn't have a favorite drink of choice. She simply enjoyed the casual act of sipping on something that reminded her of the season. And he learned her response was always some version of; I'll *have what you're having.*

So, Ethan poured two glasses of eggnog and moved them to the coffee table, then waited. As he did, his eyes got lost in the flames, and his mind got lost in thought. He didn't even hear the creak in the floor as Jade hovered in the doorway of the den.

"I wasn't sure you'd be here."

Ethan sat up and turned his body when he heard Jade's voice. He didn't know what to say, so he only nodded.

When he did, Jade carefully stepped into the room. Cautious, as if her movements were representative of her words. Like any quick or harsh motions could be interpreted as combative.

Ethan watched as she finally made it to the chair across from him and sat. Her eyes slipped to the glass of eggnog that had been poured and set on her side of the table. That's when her lip twitched ever so slightly. If he hadn't been staring at her, he never would have noticed.

"Figured we'd need these." Ethan nodded to the glass.

She didn't fidget; she just sat and studied this serious side of him that she hadn't seen before.

He wondered what she was looking for? Was she looking for a sign in him that he was still upset? Or was she waiting to muster up the courage to say something – anything?

When she spoke, it wasn't at all what he expected.

"I'm sorry."

Ethan blinked. He heard Jade apologize, but he wasn't ready for it, and he didn't need it. He didn't require her apology. He didn't *want* her apology.

Rather than acknowledge her words, Ethan explained why her apology didn't matter.

"You were right," Ethan said, earning a look of confusion from Jade.

"Sorry?" she asked after a moment, hoping for clarification.

"Earlier," he started. "You were right for what you said earlier."

"Oh, Ethan. No." Jade looked down. "I wasn't."

"You were." He put an end to her argument.

Ethan sipped his drink, then leaned forward to rest his elbows on his knees to stare at the fire.

Then he looked at her, and she hadn't moved a single muscle. She looked like she would have waited forever for him to speak.

"Why did you want to become a journalist?" he asked. "A news anchor?"

Ethan watched the surprise at his question register with Jade. There was a look that flickered across her face that told him she thought about putting up her guard – or giving him a generic answer that would have satisfied a passing stranger. But her look shifted from the poised, practiced look he'd seen on her morning show into something genuine.

"My grandma," Jade said when she finally answered. She looked down and played with the drink she was cradling in her hands. "My grandma wrote for the local newspaper. She wrote during a time when it was unusual for women to have a job outside of the home. But she was curious. And to be honest, she and my grandpa needed the extra money."

Jade grinned at the story she had heard so many times growing up that she was now sharing. It had been years since she'd even thought of it. "But," she continued, "I like to think even if they hadn't needed the money, she would have done it anyway. She loved it."

Jade took a sip of her eggnog as her eyes bore into Ethan.

"I remember thinking I wanted to be just like her. The first time I had that thought, I couldn't have been older than five – maybe six."

Ethan grinned as he imagined Jade as a five-year-old. The same feisty, driven blonde who knew what she wanted from practically the moment she was born.

"I suppose," Jade continued as she looked down, "that's a part of why all of this, here, was so tough to swallow." Jade moved her hand in a circle, but she wanted him to know she meant the house, the money, the extravagant lifestyle. It was all so different from her grandma's previous life that she had to work so hard to maintain.

Rather than let Jade go down a path he wasn't sure they'd recover from – at least on this night – Ethan decided to make his point.

"You knew as a kid what you wanted to do. You found your role model and were lucky enough – and curious enough – to make it work. To let it become a dream of your own. And all of that is great."

Ethan stopped for a moment. Then he sighed.

"I know it's hard for you not to judge or say things aloud that somebody, as driven as you, couldn't possibly comprehend, but not everybody knows what they want to do."

Ethan shook his head but kept his focus on Jade.

"The truth is, I don't know what I want to do. But, I can tell you, I know what I *don't* want to do. I don't want to end up trapped between four walls. I know I need to be outside, or I'll go crazy. So yeah, it's easy to turn my dad down when he offers to give me an office or desk. Even if it strains our relationship."

There was so much more he could say. And now that he was saying it, it all seemed so easy.

"I went to school. I earned a degree that gets me the occasional consulting gig. I'm good at it, and I make good money doing it. But it's not something I want to do eight hours a day, five days a week. What I am guilty of, though, is not actively pursuing a new job. But *you're right*. My parents did the right thing. They should have cut me off. They probably should have cut me off a long time ago. But I think they knew I wasn't ready. So, they didn't push, and I took advantage of the freedom."

Ethan took a breath.

"So, there you have it. I'm here because I had no other options. But I'm committed to seeing this through. To see what happens when it's all over. But, while I'm here, you might find me trying to figure a couple of things out – and some of that figuring might be a little harder on me than others."

Jade gave a small, supportive smile.

Ethan returned the gesture. "I guess I'm telling you all of this so I can ask for a little favor. I'll figure it out. I always do. But, in the meantime, go a little easy on a guy who's realizing his free-riding bachelor days are over?"

Jade nodded. "That," she said, "I can do."

"Okay then."

"Okay," she repeated.

Without saying another word, Ethan leaned forward to pick up *A Christmas Carol,* opened it to where the little Christmas bookmark was holding their page, and started reading from where they'd left off.

CHAPTER 18

The next morning, Jade was grateful for the call from Deni. The texts back and forth were okay, but she liked hearing her sister's voice.

"Did you get the invitation?" Jade asked once her sister was through with her customary singing greeting.

"I did. I can't wait. And, who knew you'd be throwing a Christmas party with Mr. Handsome Mountain Man over there."

Jade laughed at the unfiltered way Deni talked about Ethan.

"Have you tried to kill him yet?" Deni asked. "Or, at least wanted to?"

"At least once a day." Jade realized that her response was more for the laugh she heard Deni let out rather than her true feelings.

"Are you going to?" Deni was playing along.

Jade hesitated. Then she couldn't believe it when she spoke the truth. "I don't think so."

"Oh my gosh."

Jade heard Deni's tone on the other end of the line, and she knew she was in trouble.

"You like him!"

"No. No, no." Jade repeated the denial. "I think he's…misunderstood. I think *I* misunderstood him."

There was a pause as silence filled the phone line between them.

"Hello?" Jade asked, wondering if she had dropped the call.

"You totally like him."

"I'm trapped with him. There's a very distinct difference. We are being cordial."

"Sure. Just like you were *being cordial* with Shawn Tucker in kindergarten when you agreed to let him kiss you so he'd give you his cherry flavored candy cane."

Jade thought about it and smiled at the memory. "Yeah, it's exactly like that. He's a means to an end."

"I don't believe you."

"You, my dear sister, can believe whatever you want. As long as I see you on Christmas Day for our party."

"I'd drive a million miles to get a look at Sexy Mountain Man." Deni's voice drifted off in her daydream. "Oh, and you, of course."

"You're incorrigible."

"Better believe it. So," Deni changed the subject. "What list are you checking twice and checking off today?"

"Oh well, let's see. We are heading to the lumber yard. And we're *not* walking, hiking, or skiing. We're using a good old-fashioned 4-wheeled vehicle. I don't think I've been more excited for something since we got here."

"You're really lowering your standards up there."

"Let's just say," Jade thought about how to explain it, "I have a new appreciation for small luxuries."

"Wow." Deni sounded genuinely surprised. "You're not kidding."

"Do you want to know what I do miss, though?"

"Aside from skyscrapers, a morning news slot, and your new condo?"

Jade rolled her eyes but grinned. "Yes, aside from all of those things."

"Of course, I want to know."

"Lattes. A delicious peppermint mocha latte." Jade swooned at the thought of a melting candy cane in a pool of rich dark chocolate. She'd even settle for spiced gingerbread.

"They don't have that up in the boondocks? Not even in that super cute little town?"

"No," Jade confirmed. "But they do have killer Christmas caramel rolls."

"I'm intrigued. What's so great about them?"

"Everything."

Ethan hovered by Jade's door as he listened to her talk to what had to be a best friend or her sister. She'd talked to her sister often, and it held the same playful tone as it had in times before.

He didn't intend to linger. But they were just so *loud.*

He could hear the voice on the other end of the phone clear as day. Almost as if they were both sitting next to each other on the bed, having a face-to-face conversation.

The view was entertaining, but the feeling was satisfying. Ethan watched as Jade flipped from her back to her stomach while holding the phone to her ear. He noticed she must have turned on the Christmas tree lights that morning because it was the only offering of light in the early morning hour.

Jade looked the part, too. She had already dressed in jeans and a bright red Christmas crewneck sweater and slid on matching Christmas socks.

Ethan listened as the natural flow of conversation slowed. He smiled and thought that he might as well have a little fun with them. Besides, he'd spied on the exchange for a while. It felt wrong not to let Jade know he was there.

"Hey, what'cha doing?" Ethan crossed his arms and leaned against the door frame. It was hard for him not to flash a smug *I heard every word of your conversation* smile.

Jade scrambled into a sitting position while still holding the phone to her ear. Then, with a deer in headlights look, she barely moved her lips as she whispered into the phone, "Shh. Stop. It's Ethan." Then she straightened. "Ethan, hello. Good morning."

"Oh my gosh! Tell him you think he's hunky!"

Ethan smiled at Jade, who rolled her eyes as she pretended Deni hadn't just yelled orders through the phone.

Jade tried to hide the conversation. "Okay, Deni. Yes, I love that Christmas movie, too. It gets me every time."

"That's not what I said. He. Is. Hunky!"

A new shout echoed through the receiver, and all Ethan could do was put a hand over his face to hide the laugh.

"Right." Jade fake laughed, pretending to have a completely different conversation than the one she was really having. "Alright then, see you at the Christmas party."

"No! Stop. Tell him what I'm saying!"

Jade plastered a forced smile on her face. "Love you, too, sis."

"I didn't say I loved you! Tell Ethan you love him!"

"Bye."

Jade quickly hung up the call while Deni was still yelling on the other end.

"How was your sister this morning?" Ethan asked, unable to resist.

Jade shrugged. "Oh, you know, she's good. Just hanging out. What are you up to?"

"Heading down to breakfast and thought we could walk down together. I didn't know you were up, but I heard you talking."

"Oh yeah?" Jade tried to be casual.

Ethan nodded. "Yup. It's good to know you're not going to kill me."

Jade's eyes flew open, and they darted at Ethan in surprise. "You heard that? Wait, I mean, crap. How did you hear that?"

"You were yelling." Ethan grinned.

"I was not yelling. We're a loud family," Jade tried to defend herself, but they *were* the loudest family.

"Not you. Deni. Deni was yelling."

Jade slapped a hand over her face. "So...you heard...?"

Satisfied with the unintentional compliments he received from Deni and the slight embarrassment he was causing Jade, Ethan smiled and said, "Every word. See you at breakfast?"

He hung around for just long enough to see Jade's jaw hit the floor. Then he turned to make his way down the stairs.

CHAPTER 19

Technically, they had joined each other for breakfast that morning. But, Jade had been so preoccupied with the conversation Ethan had overheard, she barely touched the scrambled eggs and toast Ethan had made.

So, by the time they made it to the lumber yard, and she was standing in the office that hovered over the wintery view, it was easy for her to pile big, sticky bites of Cindy's Christmas caramel rolls into her mouth as she watched Ethan from above.

Jade took a bite, chewed, and stared.

Ethan was standing out in the snow in his thick winter work attire, paying close attention to one of the yardmen, and looking like he was hanging on every word.

Occasionally, Ethan and his teacher would stop, laugh, then carry on for a bit before returning their focus to a massive conveyor that was sending long strips of wood back and forth through the planer until it came out in the shape of a perfectly smooth rectangle.

While still staring, she reached two sticky fingers back toward the plate, but Jade realized the caramel roll was gone when they hit an empty plate. The moment was enough to pull her eyes away from Ethan. Her eyes grew as she realized she'd eaten the entire thing.

"Last time I saw somebody finish one of Cindy's roll's that fast was the day I saw my wife for the first time."

Jade froze when she realized she wasn't alone in the office. At some point, Jeb had climbed the steps and moved into the office, all without Jade noticing. She blinked and turned toward him.

"Sorry?" she asked, not entirely having followed Jeb's story.

Jeb pointed to Jade's empty plate, then out the window toward Ethan. "Your caramel roll, and Ethan out there." Jeb started. "Looked just like I felt the first time I saw my wife. Didn't have a clue in the world that anything else was going on around me. Matter of fact, I was eating one of Cindy's rolls at that time, just like you are now."

"Huh." It was all Jade could process with the strange feelings and ideas warming the pit of her stomach. It might have been only fifty degrees in that tiny office, but it could have been fifteen, and she wouldn't have felt even the slightest chill.

Jade didn't see Jeb's quick laugh at her shock, but she did hear him when he asked what her plan for the day was and when he told her his own.

"I need to head into town for a bit this afternoon. If you're tired of hanging around here, I'm happy to drive you in, then drop you off at the Brock residence after an hour or two."

Jade thought about a nice change of scenery and the idea of being in the town where she could wander in and out of the shops. Maybe she'd even find a Christmas present or two for her family.

"Yeah," Jade said after a moment. "I'd like that. Do you have a second for me to run down and let Ethan know?"

"You bet. I'll be down in five?" Jeb asked.

"Sounds great."

Jade walked to the door, then leaned over to sneak one last uninterrupted glance at Ethan. She couldn't possibly have been looking at Ethan like Jeb had looked at his wife. Could she?

Jade's thoughts lingered on Ethan as she walked down the old wooden steps and as she turned to walk toward where he was working.

"Jade," Ethan said her name as she approached. "Have you seen this? Isn't it something?"

Jade studied his face and slowly let Ethan's words and his excitement register. When he gave her a questioning look, she shook herself out of her trance.

"Right," she said. "Yes, I was watching from the office. Pretty amazing."

Jade watched as Ethan lifted a single brow. She tried to recover by casually tossing her thumb over her shoulder, hoping she was pointing in the general direction of the town.

"Jeb is heading into town, and I'm thinking about going with him to walk around and do a little shopping. Do you want to come?" Jade asked.

Ethan looked torn. Jade's head tilted a bit as she realized Ethan might want to stay.

"You know," she continued. "I'm just going to hop in and out of some shops, so, if you want to, you should stay. Jeb offered me a ride home."

"You're sure you wouldn't mind if I stuck around?" Ethan asked.

"Not at all. I'll just see you at home. I'll get dinner started." Jade couldn't believe how normal their conversation felt.

Ethan smiled and nodded. "Yeah, that sounds great. See you at home."

When he repeated her words, Jade felt another round of warmth cloak her body.

Jade wanted to say something else, to keep talking. Or, maybe to offer Ethan a compliment or comment on how much he seemed to be enjoying himself at the lumber yard. But Jeb was too quick to join them.

"Alright, Ms. Conner. Ready?"

So, all Jade did was offer Ethan a smile and a small wave, then turn toward Jeb. "I am."

Ethan watched Jade and Jeb walk away until he was interrupted.

"How long have you two been together? Married?"

The question caught Ethan off guard, but it made him laugh a bit at the idea.

"We're not. Actually," Ethan stole one last glance behind him where Jade was walking away, "I'm pretty sure she hates me." Then he mumbled to himself which scratching his head, "Or, at least she used to."

Three hours later, Ethan was still working, still learning. He had planed boards, chipped bark, helped fix a broken saw, and when Jeb returned, he had gotten a quick overview of the lumber yard's operations.

"So, you operate by yourselves out here?" Ethan asked.

"Sure. Once we get the orders from corporate, we are on our own. Then, once we fulfill the order, we just report back to the office – where your dad works – when we're done."

Ethan nodded. He understood perfectly.

"We rely on each other – corporate and the yard – but at the end of the day, it's on us to put in the work out here to make sure the job gets done."

"I know this isn't going to do the work justice, but it's all pretty cool," Ethan said.

Jeb laughed and said, "I know exactly what you mean. There's something about spending the day outdoors, working hard, and seeing the fruits of your labor. It's not every day you can find a job like this anymore." Jeb took a moment to sip from the pop he'd been nursing all afternoon. "Matter of fact, the job's about to be available." Jeb looked at Ethan, then let his voice take on a leading tone. "I'm getting ready to retire at the end of the month. Taking Christmas off then never looking back."

"You're retiring?" Ethan asked.

Jeb laughed again. "My wife's been nagging at me to stop working and start carting her around on road trips she's been planning for years."

Ethan smiled and held out his hand to offer Jeb a congratulatory shake. "Well, congratulations. That's really something."

"It is." Jeb followed Ethan's gaze as it traveled the length of the lumber yard. "Seems like you've got a knack for this."

Ethan looked at Jeb. "Yeah, I guess I do. I enjoy it."

"You know," Jeb started, holding Ethan's attention. "They haven't found anybody to replace me yet. With your dad at corporate, you know about the business enough. You've got the skills to be here. What if you stuck around for a bit, helped manage things until they got somebody new in? We've got enough time for me to show you the ropes. If you're interested."

Ethan didn't answer. He just nodded as he considered the question.

CHAPTER 20

Jade had spent the early afternoon wandering through town. She took time to enjoy the festive wreaths on doors and lampposts, the lights wrapped around the sidewalk trees, and the happy feeling of Christmas that seemed to find her everywhere.

She popped into a few stores and bought her mom, dad, and Deni a few Christmas gifts, then she enjoyed a coffee on a cold bench and watched the townspeople smile and laugh as they went on about their day.

Jade knew that some were taking lunch breaks, some were starting shifts or just leaving them, but as she watched everybody interact and move from one place to another, it seemed as if they all were enjoying themselves.

Was it just this special time of the year that made a regular workday seem more enjoyable? Like some magic feeling blew in with the cold weather and made every day seem like Christmas? Or did she feel like that because she had finally slowed down enough to enjoy it?

Even as she walked through the grocery store, Jade felt a sense of peace. She was calm but excited. She couldn't remember the last time she had wandered the aisles of a store, enjoying herself as she searched for ingredients to make a savory winter meal. As Christmas music happily jingled in the background, Jade wondered, when was the last time she had made dinner for herself, much less anybody else, that took longer than fifteen minutes?

Yes, the time in town had been glorious. Just what Jade had needed. But it was time to get to work.

Now, as she hovered over the vast kitchen island with carrots, potatoes, sweet potatoes, and a hefty chuck roast, she felt she was able to take a breath. And not just to breathe, but a breath that she realized could only come when you didn't feel rushed. The kind you could take when there were no demands or responsibilities looming over your head or when you weren't constantly worried about how you were going to *get ahead.*

For the first time in a long time, she could just *be.*

And, Jade thought as she looked around, it helped that she was surrounded by endless Christmas decorations, trees, twinkle lights, and the luxurious winterberry scent wafting from a candle she purchased in town.

Jade felt utterly peaceful.

Until her phone rang.

Jade leaned across the counter and checked the ID.

"Serena?" Jade questioned aloud, wondering why Serena would be calling her. They didn't have a reason to connect, especially since Jade had ended her employment early when she decided to come to her grandma's house. There hadn't been a reason to prolong her termination.

"Hello?" Jade answered the phone and leaned her hip against the counter.

"Hey, Jade. It's Serena. How are you doing?"

Jade thought the question sounded a little more involved than casual banter. It sounded a little like, *How are you doing now that your dreams have been ripped from you and you're stowed away in Middle of Nowhere, Minnesota?*

Jade laughed a bit at her own interpretation and felt a sense of relief when she didn't feel as terrible as she thought she would. Sure, it still stung, but with every passing day, it was getting better.

"Serena, hi. I'm actually doing pretty good. You caught me at a moment where I've been enjoying the ability to take a little breath."

Literally, Jade thought.

"Oh, good. I'm glad I'm catching you at a good time. And to hear that you're doing so, *so* well."

So, so well. Jade didn't know if she'd go that far. But she'd take it.

"Thanks. How are you? What has you calling today? Do you need something from me? Missed paperwork, HR stuff?" Jade wondered as she thought back to all the papers she'd signed and sent back.

"Actually, that's why I'm happy you're well."

There was a long pause on the other end of the line.

Jade looked around as if her confusion would encourage Serena to keep talking. When she didn't, Jade asked, "Serena? Are you there?"

"Yes, sorry. I am trying to find the right way to let you know. I wanted you to hear it from me rather than see it on the news."

Oh my gosh. Jade immediately knew why Serena was calling.

"Jade, they've named your replacement."

Jade's stomach fell to the floor. "Don't tell me."

"Jade, I'm so sorry."

Jade sprinted to the living room off the kitchen and fumbled with the remote as she checked her watch.

Five-oh-three.

While cradling the phone between her cheek and shoulder, Jade used two hands on the remote and targeted the TV. Then she hammered the digits on the remote. *0-0-1.*

When the screen flipped, Jade's hands fell, and the phone slipped out of its hold and thumped on the soft carpet.

"Jade?"

She heard Serena's distant voice through the phone that was lying on the ground, but nothing could have been louder than the obnoxious voice of Nick Knight staring at her from the Cities One news station, in the prime-time slot that was supposed to be hers.

Nick laughed on-screen, and Jade mimicked the terrible sound. Then she bent over, picked up her phone, and said, "Serena, thank you. I have to go." Then she clicked to end the call.

Jade stood for a while, then she side-stepped toward the couch and sat without removing her eyes from the screen.

"Of all the people," Jade whispered to herself as she watched what should have been her new co-anchors chumming it up with their new on-screen pal.

Traitors.

She probably shouldn't have, but she watched for the full thirty minutes. And with every passing minute, her irritation grew.

It's not that she particularly *wanted* the job anymore, especially since they'd replaced her with Nick. But something about it just ticked her off. She'd been passed up by a know-it-all jock with a good butt. It felt like somebody sharpened a candy cane and stuck it straight into her heart.

Jade pushed up from the couch and stomped toward the kitchen. She stared at the time and the meal she thought she was going to make.

In one long swipe across the counter, Jade used her arms to shove all of the fresh vegetables and roast to the side of the island.

"New plan," she said angrily.

She marched to the fridge and yanked it open as glass bottles clanked with the force.

"I'm home!"

Jade slowly peeked her head around the fridge door and eyed the entry into the kitchen. Her yell sounded angry and pointed. "In the kitchen!"

She reached into the refrigerator and started jerking things from their shelves and drawers. She pulled the milk and eggs from the door, wrenched bacon from the meat drawer, and slapped at the butter as she swung her hand toward the middle shelf.

Cradling all of the ingredients in her arms, she flung the door shut with her elbow just as Ethan tentatively poked his head around the corner.

When she scowled at him, he took the final brave step inside. She watched as he took inventory of the meat and veggies lying useless on the edge of the counter, then moved his gaze toward the giant bowl and mess of fridge contents she'd dropped next to it.

"What's got your Christmas undies in a bundle?" Ethan asked.

"Nothing." Jade jammed a measuring cup into the bag of flour she'd pulled from the pantry. Then she added, "And you shouldn't care if my *undies* are Christmas undies or otherwise."

Ethan pinched his lips together at her reprimand, and as half of the flour hit the counter rather than the bowl with her angry movements.

She slapped, scooped, and tossed more ingredients into the bowl before Ethan dared to ask his next question.

"What, did you get passed over for another job?"

It was meant to be a joke. But when Jade slowly pointed angry eyes at Ethan, she saw that he realized he'd come pretty close to hitting the mark.

"Oh," Ethan said when her look lasered through him. "What happened?" His tone shifted from funny to concerned.

It was enough at least to have Jade's irritation pointed back in the right direction – which was any direction away from Ethan.

When Jade said nothing and just continued hammering a wooden spoon crazily in the bowl, pausing only to crack eggs and add milk and vanilla, Ethan tried a different approach.

"What are we having for dinner?"

"Breakfast."

Jade watched Ethan as he nodded at her progress. And, because he looked like he didn't know what else to do, she kept her eyes on him as he slowly started working around her.

First, he put the milk and eggs back into the fridge. Then took a pan out for the bacon – which he must have assumed needed frying. Finally, he moved to the pantry and came out with a small box and some sprinkles.

He tried for a leading question. "This is?" He pointed a finger toward the bowl she was beating to death.

"Pancakes."

Ethan nodded and opened the box. Then he handed her a little red tube.

Jade stopped and looked at it.

"What?" he asked. "If we're having pancakes, I want Christmas pancakes."

Reluctantly Jade slid the bowl in his direction and let him place four drops of food coloring into the batter. Then she whipped it some more.

Finally, Ethan pulled up a stool to sit across from Jade and just waited.

"Nick Knight," Jade said the name with disgust.

Ethan tilted his head. "The sports dude? Jumps into freezing lakes?"

Jade plastered on a smile. "The one and only."

"Oh no," Ethan said when he finally understood. "He's your...?"

"Yeah. Just say it. *Replacement.*"

Jade stopped stirring as she tried to gather her thoughts. "You know, it's not so bad getting passed over. But getting passed over for a scummy, scuzzy, round-reared jock? It stings a little."

Jade made fast, frustrated circles with the spoon that had pancake batter flying out of the bowl. When it smacked her face, the surprise stopped her movements.

Not knowing what would happen next and not risking his own pride – or dinner – Ethan wisely covered his smile and laugh.

When Jade saw Ethen use every ounce of willpower he had to control himself, she couldn't resist the urge to laugh herself.

At first, it came in the form of a little snort. Then, when Ethan broke at the sound, Jade let herself go.

Before they knew it, both Jade and Ethan were cracking up at the moment, bending over from the aches in their sides and wiping tears from their eyes.

Ethan stood up and moved around the counter, still laughing but gathering himself. Then, Jade watched as he did the most unexpected thing. He stood in front of her and opened his arms.

When she stood and gave him a funny look, he just wiggled his fingers and said, "Come on. I know you don't want to, but just bring it in here."

For added effect, Jade stared as Ethan wiggled his fingers one more time and nodded, answering her skepticism.

With her arms flat to her sides, Jade took tiny steps forward and reluctantly walked into Ethan's chest. As she made contact, his arms came barreling around her and squeezed her tight.

After she laughed and let out a grunt at being squished, his arms loosened, and they settled into a hug.

Jade closed her eyes when the tears welled up in them, and she just let him hold her until all of the things she was upset about came and went.

After a minute, Jade sniffed, then mumbled into Ethan's chest. "You're a good hugger."

Ethan let out a quick laugh and pulled Jade back to look at her face. With his hands on her shoulders, he dipped down to check on her.

Following a quick analysis, Ethan said, "Something tells me you're going to be more than okay."

Jade sniffed once more and wiped her hand across her face. When she did, she smeared the pancake batter over her cheek and on her hand. That's when a devious look fell upon her face, and she grinned wickedly up at Ethan.

When it registered what Jade intended to do, Ethan held her at arm's length and stammered, "Oh no. Don't you dare. Don't even think about it." Ethan backed away, but he was too slow.

Jade lunged forward and caught Ethan's cheek with the batter.

"You didn't."

"Oh, I did." Jade's grin was filled with mischief.

She tried to jump at him again, but this time he caught her wrists and held them high. Both of them were laughing hard as they pushed against one another.

Finally, Jade couldn't press anymore. Her laughter had become too strong, and she needed to gain her composure.

They stood there for a moment until Ethan loosened his grip. When he let her wrists fall, he didn't bring his hand back to his sides. Instead, he brought it to Jade's face, and with the backside of his finger, he wiped away the rest of the pancake batter.

Jade paused, unsure of how to react to the tender moment.

Should she laugh? Should she close her eyes? Should she back away?

She wondered about all of those things, but none of them happened. Instead, she'd been rendered immobile and speechless. So, she looked Ethan in his eyes until he finished gently wiping her cheek.

"There," Ethan said when his arm was safely by his side. Then he asked, "You'll be okay?"

Jade nodded. And when her mind allowed for it, she thought about his question. She thought about the job she'd lost and who she'd lost it to. But she also remembered the sense of happiness and peace she'd felt that day.

Still nodding, Jade looked up. "Yeah, I'll be okay."

"Good. Now, let's make some pancakes. I have something to tell you. It was an interesting day at the lumber yard."

CHAPTER 21

Ethan had asked Jade if she wanted to stay and watch TV with him. To unwind after their day. But something about the day she'd had – the happy feeling of Christmas she'd felt in town, sharing an unexpected moment with Ethan in the kitchen, then listening as Ethan told her that he'd been offered a temporary job at the lumber yard while they shared bright red Christmas pancakes – all of it had her wanting to retreat to her room for a little bit.

When Jade walked in, she didn't even bother with the overhead light. Instead, she walked to the tree and bent down to plug it in. Then she sat back as the glow from the Christmas lights lit up her room.

Jade sat on the floor for a little while, but something about the quiet contentment had her reaching for the box of letters.

Jade decided to stay next to the tree, so she scooted backward until her back was against the wall.

Then she placed the old box on her lap, carefully lifted the top, and gently set it aside.

Since she didn't know where to start, for a little while, she just thumbed through the letters, occasionally pulling one out a bit, then sliding it back into place so she could do the same with another. When she reached the end of the box, she gently ran her fingers down the tops of the letters until they rested on the first one.

Jade carefully pulled it from the envelope and started reading.

December 17, 1942

My Love,

You always told me I was lucky. And as luck would have it, I won the lottery.

Turns out next month, I'm headed off to training camp. From there, I'll probably head to Japan. But, I suppose, no one really knows.

I won't see you for Christmas this year. It's hard to imagine it will be our first Christmas apart in four years.

All I keep thinking about is our parents telling us we were crazy. Turns out the only thing I'm crazy about is you.

We'll celebrate soon, My Love. Until then, I'll think of you often.

Always Yours, Lenny Brock

Jade brought a hand to her face as her wide eyes stared at the letter.

"It couldn't possibly be," Jade whispered. Could the letter have been written to her grandma?

Jade quickly folded the letter, gently placed it back in the envelope, and reached into the box for the next letter.

At first, she didn't read them. She just moved from one letter to the next, looking at the dates and who the letters were written to.

"Nineteen-forty-two, *My   Love.* Forty-three, forty-four, forty-five." Jade rambled as she checked one letter then another, all written to the same *My Love.*

Then she found one.

December 24, 1949

Dear Sweet Helen,

I suppose it's not my right to call you My Love anymore. When I was discharged and got back home, I heard the happy news that you're to be wed.

My Love (I just had to say it one more time), I wish you joy. You are joy. I wish I could be there to see you in that wedding dress.

Not much going on here, just learning how to chop wood. I always thought you'd like it out here in the country. Maybe one day you and your new husband can visit – I'd love to have you.

Always Yours, Lenny Brock

Tears flooded Jade's eyes. She held the letter to her chest and hugged it as all of her overdue emotions came pouring out.

She heaved and ached at the memory of losing her grandpa, then again at being so angry with her grandma when she decided to remarry. And finally, she cried for the love that her grandma and Lenny had shared so long ago before a war had stolen it from them.

How was it possible one box could so suddenly shift everything she thought she knew?

Jade pulled the letter away from her body, stared at it once more, then folded it.

She wiped her eyes and decided she needed more time. She wanted to keep the letters to herself, just for a little bit. She wasn't ready to share them without knowing what was written in them. She wanted to know her grandmother's story through the eyes of Lenny Brock. Through the eyes of a man she was now mourning because she hadn't taken the time to know him.

Tomorrow, she thought. Tomorrow she'd get up early, pour herself a coffee, and she would start from the beginning. Because tonight, she wanted to be with Ethan. She wanted to sit with him in the den and listen as he read the last pages of *A Christmas Carol.* She wanted to sit by the warmth of the fire, with the white lights of the Christmas tree adding a glow to the dim, intimate room. She wanted to share these moments with him because she realized she was going to miss them when they were over.

Jade changed into her flannel pajamas as she usually did before she headed down. She took the time to brush out her hair, then tie it in a long, twisting braid that draped over the side of her shoulder. She took one last look at the letters sitting beneath the Christmas tree, then turned and walked out of the room.

CHAPTER 22

"Do you want to walk a bit before I drop you off at the lumber yard?" Jade asked Ethan while licking caramel off her fingers in Cindy's diner.

Ethan's quick grin had her smiling back.

"What?" she asked before letting him respond. "You know they're the best."

Of course, she was referring to the Christmas caramel rolls. If the window of availability was only during the Christmas season, she was going to enjoy them as often as possible.

"Yes," Ethan said. "To both of those things. Should we go now?"

Jade nodded and pushed away from the table, then led Ethan toward the door while they draped themselves in warm winter gear.

The day was clear and sunny, but as all beautiful bright winter days are, it was deceptively cold. The air had a chill to it they hadn't yet felt that winter, and the wind held a bite to it as it nipped at their faces. But it didn't take away from their pleasure.

"Have you thought more about the offer from Jeb?" Jade asked as her breath came out in thick white puffs in front of her face.

Ethan wore gloves but still hid his hands in his pockets for the extra warmth. And he ducked his face behind the high collar of his winter coat before responding. "I have. Thought about it, I mean."

"And?" Jade asked, wanting to know how he felt about it.

Ethan glanced at Jade. "And, I think I'm going to do it." He gave a hint of a shrug. "I like the idea of helping out."

Jade's smile was genuine. She had noticed the energy in him from the first time they'd set foot on the lumber yard.

Admittedly, she had been so preoccupied with her own situation she hadn't realized it at the time, but he seemed to like it. He loved the outdoors. He loved the hard, physical work. He definitely enjoyed the comradery she had seen between him and the other yardmen.

"Do you feel good about it?" Jade asked but followed it up with a more pointed question. "In here, I mean?" she pointed a gloved hand at his chest.

Ethan laughed a bit self-consciously, but he nodded. "Yeah, I guess I do."

"Then, I think we have reason to celebrate. How about tonight we actually eat that roast?"

"On a day like today, I can't think of coming home to anything better."

Jade felt the heat burn her cheeks. It caused a tingle as the warmth fought the bitter cold.

"Good," she said. Then she stopped and held out her arm to stop Ethan with her. "Look. Do you see that?"

"The Winter Festival? Yeah, the guys at the yard have been talking about it nonstop."

"No," Jade said. "Not that. Look."

She nodded toward a news crew with cameras and lights shining on the adorable pregnant news anchor.

"Let's go watch!" The excitement in Jade was immediate. She grabbed Ethan's arm and dragged him across the slick pavement to the other side of the road.

The crew had set up right in front of a twenty-foot Christmas tree lighting up the center of town. It was the perfect spot for a holiday segment.

Jade beamed as she felt the pure joy emulating from the anchor.

As the story seemed to be winding down, Ethan leaned over and whispered to Jade. "Are you crying?" He asked the question playfully, but inside said a silent prayer that they were tears of joy.

Jade sniffled. "Yes. She's wonderful. And she looks so happy. What do you see when you look at her?" Jade asked Ethan.

Out of the corner of her eye, she saw Ethan turn and study the woman. "Honestly?"

"Yes."

"I see a woman who looks like she's going to have a baby any minute. But," Ethan continued at Jade's elbow jab. "Yeah, I think she seems happy."

"She must love the job," Jade commented, not expecting a response.

"Or, she loves what she's talking about. Or the town. Or she knows she's about ready to have a baby and take the next four months off."

"Very funny. *But,*" Jade moved her head back and forth, considering his assessment, "you might not be entirely wrong."

When the cameras stopped rolling, Jade and Ethan began to turn. It was past the time Jade should have dropped Ethan off at the lumber yard, and she had some housekeeping items she wanted to tend to now that the Christmas party was getting closer. But as the woman finished her piece, she frantically started waving her arms in Jade and Ethan's direction.

They both looked behind them to see who's attention she was trying to grab. But the closer she got, Jade realized she was waving to *them.*

"Hi! Hello-hi!" The greetings flew out of the beautiful woman's mouth as she waddled over. "It's Jade. I mean, you're Jade Conner."

Ethan raised an eyebrow in Jade's direction. She caught it when she glanced his way, wondering if she should know this woman.

"I'm Emily Anders. I'm a local journalist. Morning anchor. Newscaster. Well, really, I'm pretty much everything around here, except for the evening news. But, *you!* You're…amazing!"

Jade felt a different type of blush return to her face. Apparently, Emily knew who she was, so the only response she could give was, "Yes, I'm Jade Conner."

"I'm so sorry. This must seem so strange. I just…well…I watched your morning show every day until I switched to mornings myself. I'm such a big fan."

Jade blinked.

"Thank you." Ethan leaned in and responded for Jade. "She says, *Thank you.*"

"Yes! My gosh, I'm sorry. Thank you. That's so nice of you to say. Um, your show...you're so wonderful."

"Thank you." Emily accepted the compliment like it was the best one she'd ever been given. "I hope this isn't strange, but would you like to join me for lunch? Not today, of course. Just sometime?"

Jade's heart melted. "I would love that." She nodded. "I would *really* love that."

Jade tried to think of the schedule she and Ethan had put together for that week.

"Tomorrow?" Ethan offered. "She's free for lunch tomorrow."

Jade's laugh held a tinge of embarrassment. But she was going to go to lunch! With a new friend! She shrugged and nodded enthusiastically.

"Tomorrow is perfect." Emily's gaze traveled back and forth between Jade and Ethan. "Should we meet at Cindy's? Say, noon?"

"I honestly can't wait. Thank you."

"Great! I should go. I'll see you tomorrow."

They watched as Emily teeter-tottered away to help her team pack up.

"Look at you," Ethan said, nudging Jade's arm. "Snow Queen, you're famous."

"Ha-ha. I'm just happy I don't have to stare at *you* over lunch tomorrow."

Ethan flung his gloved hands over his heart and faked a shot to the chest. "Ouch, it hurts." Ethan stuttered a step or two as if he was about to fall from the blow Jade had given him.

She shoved him playfully, then said, "You're ridiculous. Come on."

Ethan laughed as he righted himself, then, without a thought, he tossed his arm over Jade's shoulder, and they walked the rest of the way back to the car, not realizing they were laughing the entire way.

CHAPTER 23

There was nothing like the feeling of being hot on a bitterly cold day. Finding that perfect balance between warm and cold. Especially when it was the result of good, hard work.

Ethan got lost in his work for the second day in a row, and he loved every minute of it.

"Seems like you're getting the hang of things around here."

Ethan stood from his crouched position by a sawmill and grinned at Jeb's voice closing in from behind. He stretched and admitted, "I've been here before. A *long* time ago. And if you would have told me that I would enjoy the work this much then, I might've told you you were nuttier than the nutcrackers lining our mantel."

Jeb laughed and nodded. "Well, I've found timing is key when it comes to most things in life. But, I'm glad you found your way here now."

Jeb hovered for a bit as they both took in the view. The combination of wilderness, industry, and winter was intoxicating. "Have you given more thought to my offer?"

Ethan squinted into the sun to look at Jeb. "Yeah, I have. I'd be honored to help out until you find a good replacement."

"Well, alright then." Jeb's excitement was evident in the pleased shoulder slap he gave Ethan. "Alright then. How long do we have with you today? I could show you a couple more things."

As Ethan wondered if he needed to get home for anything, he heard Jade's voice call from the parking lot.

"Hey guys, how's it going today?"

Ethan and Jeb turned to see a peppy Jade walking toward them.

Ethan felt his smile grow at the sight of Jade's satisfied grin and wondered if she would notice?

"Hey," Ethan said. "Just the Snow Queen we were hoping to see. Do we have anything on the docket for this afternoon?"

Jade shook her head. "Not a thing. In fact, that's why I stopped by. I thought I could leave the car for you. I just finished lunch with Emily Anders."

"Emily Anders? You've met?" Jeb asked, seeming happy with the connection made.

"Just yesterday," Jade admitted. "She's like…a breath of fresh air. Such a nice person. We had so much fun over lunch we planned another for next week."

Jeb raised his eyebrows and said, "If she doesn't have a new baby by then."

"You're not kidding. She's ready." Jade turned to Ethan. "But, she's also stepping in on the local evening news tonight. I came by to see if you wanted to watch it with me? Would you be finished here by four-thirty?"

Ethan looked at Jeb. "What do you think, boss?"

"Plenty of time. Though I can't remember the last time I made it a point to watch the news."

Ethan grinned. "Well, she loves it." He looked to Jade. "Looks like it's a date. Are you sure you don't want the car?"

"No, you take it."

"I'm sure I can find somebody to give you a ride up the road. Let me see if anybody's heading that way," Jeb offered.

Both men watched as Jade brushed it off. "Thanks, Jeb. But I'm good. I threw an extra pair of boots in the trunk and some good cold-weather hiking gear. I think I'll walk back. Besides, if I don't, Cindy's Christmas caramel rolls are going to start showing up in places where rolls don't belong."

"Really?" Ethan asked, surprised that Jade would make the unnecessary decision to trek through the snow when she had a perfectly functioning car. He tilted his head and studied her. There was something in her that was shifting. She seemed more carefree. More...happy. "Okay," he said finally. "Text me when you get home to let me know you made it?"

Jade angled her face at his request, and suddenly he wondered if it wasn't his place to bother? But he wanted to bother. He wanted her to get home safely. And – he couldn't believe what he was thinking – he *wanted* to get home to watch the news with her.

Ethan blinked as he tried to process his new state of mind. But, it seemed that his new state of mind seemed to mostly revolve around Jade.

The exercise had felt good. *Almost* as good as the hot shower she'd get to take when she'd finally made it back. But, what felt better than all of that, was the idea that Ethan was waiting for a text from her.

He cared if she made it home safely.

Two weeks ago, she was pretty sure he would have hoped for her to get lost along the way or gobbled up in an avalanche.

Jade giggled to herself a bit at the thought and how different things were between them. She was looking forward to the evening. To watch the news, sure, but the idea that she'd get to share another dinner, another moment, with Ethan was the best part.

Unfamiliar with the landscape, Jade mostly stuck to the road she and Ethan had driven on their first night at the house together, so getting home took a bit longer than she intended. But, she didn't want to chance the snowy terrain by herself. She'd leave that for the next time she and Ethan went out together.

Jade indulged in an extra-long shower, and it was glorious. But now, she had less time to get downstairs and throw a nice TV dinner together.

Ethan had mentioned that he liked chili, and all that took was a bit of chopping and about an hour of cooking time. So, she'd show him *chili*. This wasn't going to be any generic canned special. In fact, after tonight, he might never eat canned chili again.

Jade skipped down the stairs and made her way to the kitchen. Rather than listening to the TV, she flipped on the radio and let the laughter of Bruce Springsteen tell her that Santa Claus was coming to town.

She chopped onions, peppers, and sweet potatoes and tossed them into a pot while humming to the tunes and moving to cheerful song after cheerful song. Before long, she had chunky tomatoes, garlic, spices, and ground beef cooking away on the stove. Then, just for fun, she shredded some cheddar cheese and danced her way to the pantry to pull out the Fritos. There were some things chili couldn't be eaten without.

Jade smiled as she thought back to Ethan and his description of chili. At the time, she hadn't told him, but she agreed, the curly corn chips were a necessity.

Since she wasn't *that* scared of the basement anymore, Jade turned on all the lights and headed down to rummage through the crawlspace to find some old tray tables. She knew her grandmother had had some, but she had no idea if they had made the move.

After five minutes of searching, Jade was pleasantly surprised to find them neatly stacked against the back wall by an endless supply of folding tables and chairs.

"Yikes," Jade said as she took inventory of the seating. Then she bit her lip as she contemplated the view. They'd probably need all of those for the Christmas party. *And,* she thought, it seemed like a job Ethan should help her with.

Jade lifted two dinner trays, one beneath each arm, and carefully climbed the stairs. Every other step, one of the trays hit a wall or the top of a stair.

Oh, to be taller, Jade thought as she grunted up the next two steps. But on cue, Ethan appeared at the top of the stairs.

"I thought I heard you down here. Here, let me help." He reached down, and grabbed the sides of each table, and hauled them up with what looked like no effort at all.

Jade rolled her eyes as she followed him the rest of the way up, but she was too grateful for the help to comment.

"I found a whole load of tables and chairs downstairs. We'll probably need them for Christmas."

"Right. Great idea. Don't try and get them up by yourself. I'll help. Or, I'll just do it. You can order me around and tell me where to put them."

Jade smiled at Ethan, who was standing holding the TV trays, ready to take orders.

"Where would you like these?"

"Hmm, let's put them in the living room."

As they moved through the kitchen and into the living room, Jade watched as Ethan closed his eyes and stopped to savor the smell.

"This, right now, is the best moment of my whole day. What is that? Chili?"

Jade beamed. "I should warn you, it's not from a can."

"I don't know if I'll ever be able to go back," Ethan said while opening his eyes.

"I had the same worry."

Ethan laughed. "I'm not sure *worry* is the right word."

While Ethan set up the tray tables next to the couch, Jade scoured the kitchen for silverware, bowls, and heavy linen napkins. They might be eating in the living room, but they were going to enjoy it.

She poured them both a cranberry-red wine, then made the final placements with ten minutes to spare.

"Ready?"

"I don't know if I've ever been hungrier. And this looks amazing. You even got Fritos."

Jade shrugged. "It's a chili staple."

"Ah, you were holding out on me."

Grinning, Jade admitted, "I couldn't have you thinking we were getting along."

When the tell-tale introduction music played – and all news stations' introductions sounded similar – Jade gasped, excited to watch Emily. "It's time! Ready?"

Ethan smiled as he spied on Jade out of the corner of his eye. He laughed a little at her excitement and shared a bit of it as well. "I can't wait."

"She was fantastic." Jade scraped her bowl with a Frito, then took a crunching chomp, completely taken with the show. "I can't wait to tell her. She was glowing. Her face lit up when she talked about the Winter Festival. The caroling, the skating, the horse and sleigh rides. It seemed like she really loved it all. But really," Jade gestured like she was stating the obvious, "who wouldn't love that?" She waved a hand forward. "Anyway, Emily is precious. And brilliant on screen. I can't get enough."

Ethan swiped a finger around the rim of his bowl and smirked as he listened to Jade talk a mile-a-minute. *Passion* was one word that came to mind. But *perfect* was another.

He felt the silly grin on his face, but he couldn't help it. Jade, the unexpected, over-the-top, passionate woman – who he was sure only weeks ago would drive him crazy – had stopped his heart. Suddenly, he knew exactly how the Grinch felt. Who knew a heart could actually grow three sizes?

Ethan gave a silent laugh at his thoughts. And, in what seemed like an instant, he wanted to know everything about her.

"What's so funny? You liked it, right?" Jade looked concerned as she took a sip of her wine.

"I loved it. Emily was great."

"But?" Jade asked, assuming there was a *but.*

"No *buts* about the show. I am curious, though, would you have changed anything? How would you have done it?"

Jade had never thought about that before. She'd always been the one to deliver the news, not create the line-up. It was an interesting question.

"I guess, I don't know."

"Give it a shot."

"Um, okay. I guess I've always thought that *breaking news* is good upfront. But during the holidays I would start with something that makes people feel happy. The sleigh story, or even the Santa puppy drive. There's always time to get to the *meat.* I think the middle is the right place for that – the meat, I mean. The heavy stuff." Jade shrugged. "But, when you're only given a half-hour, I think it should be an obligation to give people the news, but also to make them feel good." Jade nodded, agreeing with herself.

Then, she looked up, surprised. "That's what I love the most about the job. It's like this home and this town. When you feel good, something in you changes. Something has changed in me."

"It looks good on you."

Ethan thought his words might surprise her, but the way she turned and looked at him, with eyes so big and so joyful – and also with a bit of shock – it was worth it.

He knew his time was short. Christmas was a little over a week away. But he didn't want to hold back. Because the truth was, he was feeling good, too.

Maybe he could surprise her once more.

"If you were with your grandma right now, what would you be doing?" The urge to learn everything about her was overwhelming.

Jade looked dazzled and frazzled. First the news question, then the compliment, then a question about her grandma.

Ethan knew he was asking a lot. She might not answer but–

"Cookies," Jade said the word lightly, easily. Like there wasn't a doubt in her mind what she and her grandma would have done on the freezing cold winter night together.

"We would turn on her oven for heat – their kitchen was *tiny!* We'd turn on the radio. We'd sing and dance. She'd ask me about boys and school and what I wanted for Christmas. We'd talk about crazy dreams. And we'd bake cookies." Jade let her shoulders rise and fall.

Ethan nodded, looked down, and thought about Jade's answer. All the while, his head bobbing up and down. "Yes. Okay, yes. Well, then, let's make some Christmas cookies."

Jade's eyes danced. "*You* want to make Christmas cookies with me?"

Ethan looked at Jade. "I want to make cookies with you." He waited a second before adding, "I want you to *teach* me how to make cookies."

"Wait," Jade said, narrowing her eyes. "You've never made Christmas cookies before?"

Ethan scratched his head. "I, um, does the kind that comes in a log count? You know? You just, like, slice off a chunk. Eat some, cook some."

Jade shook her head and smiled as a twinkle played in her eyes. "Oh no, that doesn't even come close to counting. How do you feel about gingerbread men?"

Ethan hemmed and hawed. "I'd say top five on a Christmas cookie list."

"Ethan Brock, that is just not acceptable. By the time we're finished, you're going to check that list and bump gingerbread right up there to number one."

Before they started, they lit all of the Christmas lights in the house. The tops of cupboards, stair banisters, and every Christmas tree in the house were sparkling. Then, they turned on the train that circled the tree in the den, shook all of the snow globes, and when they finally made their way back to the kitchen, they flicked off the TV and turned on the radio.

Jade guided, and Ethan worked. He creamed, whipped, mixed, tasted, rolled, and cut out gingerbread men the size of his head.

While the cookies baked, Ethan held out his hand, and he spun Jade around the kitchen to *Rockin' Around the Christmas Tree,* then slowed and swayed her to *Oh Holy Night.*

As the song came to an end, their bodies stopped moving, but they didn't part.

Ethan held on. Jade didn't back away.

When Ethan took a breath. He didn't know what he wanted to say, but he felt he had to say something.

But before he could, the blaring sound of the kitchen timer had them jumping apart like they'd just been caught doing something off-limits.

Their embarrassed laughs lasted only a second because instead of staying in the moment, Jade rushed around the island to the timer to stop the buzzing. She busied herself with putting on a bright red oven mitt and pulling the cookies out.

All Ethan could do was feel the cold hit his body where her warmth used to be as he watched her rush around the kitchen. He wanted that moment again. He wanted her back in his arms. He needed another night like this one.

With Jade's back still facing him, he asked, "Do you want to join me at the Christmas festival this weekend?"

CHAPTER 24

It was their first Christmas festival together, so naturally, they decided to go all out.

"Are you ready?" Jade yelled from around the corner of the den where Ethan was waiting for her.

"Only if you are."

"Oh," Jade popped out from around the corner, "I am ready!"

Ethan's laugh was instant. "Are those reindeer elves?"

"With jingle bell shoe pompoms," Jade said the words like Ethan had missed the most essential feature of her seriously ugly Christmas sweater.

Then, to give Ethan his very own private show, she shimmed, and the sweater obnoxiously jingled to life.

Ethan covered his mouth and stared. "It's…perfect."

"Well, alright. How come you're hiding? Out with it." Jade motioned to Ethan, who had been wearing a blanket, when she jumped into the room.

She expected an elaborate show, maybe one shoulder at a time, or a clever peek-a-boo act. Instead, Ethan flung the blanket off in a single, confident disrobe.

The snort that escaped Jade's mouth as she took in the ridiculous outfit had her hands flying to her mouth.

She watched as Ethan stretched his arms out to give her a full, spinning view of the magnificence of his sweater.

"You're…an actual reindeer."

Ethan furrowed his eyebrows, clearly disappointed with her assessment. "Excuse me." Ethan turned to show off the butt and bushy tail protruding from the back of his shirt, then spun and pointed to the red, glowing nose that sat on the mounted reindeer head. "I am not just *any* reindeer. I am Rudolf. He's arguably the most famous reindeer of all."

Jade pinched her lips together as she listened. She nodded while doing her best not to crack up and ruin his moment. "It's just...you're…*you*, are wonderful. Truly."

She couldn't hold it in anymore. The laughter billowed out, and when Ethan turned his head and got poked in the face by a foam antler rack, all control was lost.

"Okay, come on, Snow Queen," Ethan said after giving Jade ample time to get her laughs in. "We've got a Winter festival to get to."

"Okay, fine, I'm coming. But really," Jade pointed a finger up and down the length of Ethan's sweater, "remarkable."

"Thank you." He accepted the compliment while ushering her out of the den.

"What's the rush?" Jade asked while Ethan worked around her, putting her stocking cap on her head and dressing her hands in thick cream-colored gloves. Jade laughed at the doting and the hurry.

Ethan spun and grabbed a blanket from a chair near the entry, and Jade gave him an amused look.

"Do you think we're going to need a blanket at the Winter Festival?" she asked, as Ethan just scooted her toward the door.

He didn't answer right away; he just opened the door and pulled her out with him. Then he said, "No, but we will for this."

When Ethan stepped to the side, Jade gasped at the magnificent horse-drawn sleigh parked before them.

"This?" Jade shook her head, then child-like bright eyes turned on Ethan. "This is what we're taking to the festival?"

Ethan offered a bow as he elegantly led her toward the beautiful, deep berry red sleigh. "One very magical outdoor activity checked off the list."

Rather than climbing aboard at his gentlemanly gesture, she threw herself in his arms. "This is just the best!"

Ethan and Jade spun with the momentum. When they slowed, Ethen held her close. He wondered what it would be like to kiss her. Could he? Did she want him to? Would she kiss him back?

He searched her eyes, hoping for a sign. Any glint or glimmer that encouraged him to try.

Then, Jade moved a little closer. She looked up and into his eyes. And that was enough. Enough for him to try. He'd regret it forever if he didn't.

Ethan moved in slowly, watching Jade's eyes the entire way. He wanted her to be sure. And when she closed hers, he knew.

"Well, how about this?"

Jade and Ethan jumped apart and spun around.

"Sully?" they both questioned at the voice they heard coming from the sleigh, then they looked at each other.

"Perfect night for a sleigh ride, don't you think?" Sully rested a hand on his leg as he turned and greeted Jade and Ethan. "Good evening," Sully smirked. "Nice to see the both of you *getting along.*"

Jade flushed, and Ethan darted his eyes toward her at Sully's subtle remark at their closeness. Then, he grinned and stepped aside, holding out his hand.

"After you," Ethan said, helping Jade onto the sleigh.

Ethan picked up the blanket that had fallen to the ground when Jade had jumped into his arms and let the small smile play at his lips as he remembered the feeling. Then he climbed into the sleigh himself and nodded at Sully. "Good evening, Sully. It's nice to see you again."

The cold wind whipped around them as the sleigh slid through the snow.

The sound of the handsome Clydesdale's hooves slapping the ground, of the snow crunching beneath them, and the warmth from the blanket and Ethan's arm around her became Jade's favorite feelings.

The sudden happiness resulted in a quick panic. Just as Jade started to settle into the feeling, thoughts and doubts about her future slammed into her. She must have stiffened because Ethan bent and put his lips next to her ear.

"Are you okay?" he asked.

The whisper warmed her cheek, and the sweet sound and sentiment had her trying to push the worry away.

This was a time to enjoy. For the first time in her life, she didn't want to think about tomorrow. She wanted to experience today. Because soon enough, they would be gone. And so would Ethan. They'd go their separate ways and move on to lead their own lives hundreds of miles apart.

"Yeah," she said. "Just trying to hold onto this moment."

Without thinking, Jade rested her head on Ethan's shoulder and closed her eyes for just a second to rid herself of doubt. Then she opened them to let the magic of the ride consume her.

"We're here," Sully said as the sleigh slowed to a stop.

It was too soon, but as they took in the little town lit up in twinkle lights, the timing seemed just right. The street was filled with laughter. Happy sounds and songs sounded from a distance where a choir sang near the Christmas tree. And everybody was wrapped in their best reds and greens.

Jade and Ethan looked at each other, hungry for the moment. Both eager to experience the town together in this new and wonderful way.

They stopped and talked with their new friends and acquaintances from the lumber yard and those they were familiar with from town. They both realized it hadn't taken them long to become a part of the community, and they wondered if it was the town or the season that lent so much to the open arms.

Throughout the night, Jade sang along with the choir to carols she didn't even know she knew the words to. Ethan kept them warm with hot cocoas and laughter. They got their faces painted with kids young and old, and they smudged the edges while wiping their faces after indulging in a late-night Christmas caramel roll.

"I can't believe I've been missing this." Jade stared at the over-the-top Christmas event, baffled at the thought. "No wonder my grandma loved it here. This would have undoubtedly been her favorite time of the year. All of these people, endless food, so much laughter, and so much happiness. It's contagious."

Ethan grinned at Jade's view of the town and the winter celebration they were all sharing together. He agreed. With every ounce of his being, he agreed with her. "It's..." As Ethan began to agree with her, his eyes squinted into the distance. "It's...Emily. And, I think she's in labor."

Jade's eyes lurched out of her head as she spun around in time to see Emily hunched over, holding a microphone and her enormous belly.

"Emily!" Jade shouted as they both ran over to her side.

By the time they neared, friends and neighbors had gathered around to help.

"Jade?" Emily grunted out the word.

Jade squeezed through a few people and knelt by Emily, letting her new friend grip her hand with all of her might. "Yes, I'm here. What can I do?" Jade asked.

"Finish," Emily said.

"Sorry, what?" Jade looked confused.

"Take the microphone, and sign off." Emily nodded toward a camera and a bright, blinding light. Then Emily pushed the microphone into Jade's hands. "Sign off." Emily smiled. "Tell everybody – in a very appealing way – that there's a baby on the way."

Jade laughed and nodded. She kissed the side of her new friend's head and said, "Don't worry about a thing. Just go bring a beautiful new baby into this world.

Within seconds of standing, Emily was whisked away and out of sight. Jade stood with the microphone close to her chest, with Ethan and the camera crew staring at her.

When Jade did nothing and looked blankly at Ethan, he mimed lifting the microphone to his mouth and whispered, "Say something."

Jade smiled at the chaos, Christmas, and the unbelievable situation she found herself in. Yet, her smile had never felt more genuine.

Jade looked at the camera and said, "This is Jade Conner, stepping in for the beautiful, soon-to-be mom, Emily Anders. Thank you for being with us tonight at the Winter Festival. I – *we* – wish you the happiest, most wonderful time of the year. Until tomorrow, Happy Holidays."

The camera rolled as Jade watched the hand of the cameraman move from one finger to zero. Then the light dimmed, and the camera was brought down.

Jade laughed and shrugged at the skinny girl behind the camera. The equipment seemed bigger than the girl herself.

"That was great!" The tiny, pixie-haired brunette said as she bounded over to Jade. "Fantastic stand-in. Leave it to Emily to make her final departure by going into labor on camera. I'm Quinn."

Jade held out her hand. "Jade Conner."

"Oh, I *know*. Emily and I are *huge* fans."

Jade couldn't believe it. Sure, at one time, she wished people would know of her. But now, hearing somebody say they were a fan seemed insignificant. *Incredible,* but no longer important.

"Well, I'm a fan of yours. I'm happy we were here. What crazy luck. And Emily!" Jade realized the impact of what was happening. Her eyes grew excited. "Emily is having her baby." Jade sighed.

"I know." Quinn seemed conflicted. Excited but let down. "She's going to be such a great mom."

Jade gave Quinn a silly grin. She didn't know the young girl well enough to read her. Maybe she just wasn't one to get over-the-top excited.

After a moment, Quinn lifted her arms. "Alright then. I suppose I should pack up and get everything back to the station. Great clip."

"Thanks," Jade said. "Merry Christmas, Quinn."

"You, too, Jade."

Jade and Ethan stood next to each other as they watched the quirky girl walk away from them.

Jade shook her head as she tried to process what had just happened. "That was…?"

Ethan hunkered toward her and said, "Fantastic!" Finishing the thought for her. "You were so cool. Just calm, collected, and awesome."

Jade blushed at the onslaught of compliments. Then she admitted, "It was really fun. I didn't realize how much I missed being in front of a camera. And getting to close out on something so exciting. It felt good."

"You belong where the world can see you."

Jade tilted her head at the sweet statement. It was the nicest, best thing anybody had ever said to her. It felt terrific, but then, Jade wondered, why did she feel a hint of sadness?

Jade was looking forward to the warmth and comfort of the den. After the energetic bustle of the Winter Festival, they were both ready for the fire, the quiet, and their time alone. What was left of their time together was becoming more precious by the day.

They'd each gone their separate ways to change into their cozy nightwear, then made their way back to each other in the den.

Jade smiled on her way back down as she thought back to the day she'd first arrived. She hadn't even wanted to share this part of her day with Ethan. Now, she was rushing to change, checking her face and hair in the mirror, then purposefully having to slow her pace on the way down the stairs.

As her hand slid along the railing, she wondered if this was how her grandma and Lenny had spent their evenings together. Had they retreated to the den every night to talk and read together?

The idea made her happy rather than sad. To know her grandma had that kind of companion made her heart swell.

Jade heard Ethan clinking around the bar in the den before she turned the corner to walk in. When he came into view, the sight of him in a vibrant, jolly green shirt and matching sweatpants had her stifling a giggle. But seeing the way he looked up and held two glasses of eggnog with a goofy grin had Jade softening. The funny-looking Santa hat he was wearing was just the cherry on top.

"I have an idea," Ethan said as he came out from behind the bar. "I know we are supposed to read something together. But we've had a long day. All of that laughing, and singing, and dancing – it's hard work."

"It really is," Jade said, sounding serious and playing along.

"What if tonight, rather than *read* a story, we watch one?" Ethan asked as he set their drinks on the coffee table and pulled out a box filled with old Christmas video cassette tapes.

"What are *those?*" Jade laughed as she peered into the box.

Ethan stood tall. "These are what the old folk call VHS tapes. They were big in the eighties and nineties."

Jade swatted a hand at Ethan's shoulder. "Hey, *I* am a product of the eighties and nineties. Who are you calling *old folk?*"

"Apologies, Snow Queen. But, what do you think?"

"I think a movie has never sounded so good."

Jade busied herself with collecting blankets and pillows for the couch while Ethan wheeled an old cart over to where they were sitting.

"A TV on a cart. I honestly never thought I'd ever see that again. It really is fascinating."

She jumped into her spot on the couch and tucked herself into the plush covers, leaving only her eggnog on the outside.

Just as Ethan settled in next to her, Jade's phone rang. She gave him a questioning look as he reached forward so he could hand it to her.

He looked at the caller ID. "It's local. Maybe you should answer?"

"Hello," Jade answered, looking at Ethan as she waited for a response on the other end.

When her eyes widened at the greeting, she quickly put the phone on speaker so Ethan could hear.

"Ah, yes, hello, Mr. Marsh."

Then Jade mouthed the introduction that Ethan missed. *He's from the local news!*

Intrigued, Ethan lifted his eyebrows and nodded, waiting for the man on the other end to talk.

"As you know, Emily Anders went into labor tonight. I regretfully don't have baby news to share with you just yet, but I was hoping to offer something else that you might consider to be good news."

Jade looked curiously at Ethan, who nodded, encouraging her to respond.

"Yes, we'd – I mean, I'd – love to hear it."

"We hadn't planned for Emily's fill-in anchor to begin until after the holidays. Ms. Conner, we were wondering if you'd be interested in a temporary morning news position?" There was a brief pause on the other end. Then Mr. Marsh added, "Tomorrow."

Jade's jaw felt like it dropped into her eggnog.

Was she just offered a job?

"Hello? Did I lose you, Jade?"

"No, no. Sorry. I'm here."

Jade looked at Ethan and lifted her shoulders slightly as if to ask, *what do you think?*

Ethan grinned, nodded, then finally gave his final answer by whispering, "Absolutely!"

Jade enthusiastically started nodding with Ethan and looking from him to the phone.

Finally, Ethan whispered again, "He can't hear your nod."

"Right!" Jade said. "Mr. Marsh, yes. Yes, I would love to fill in. When do you need me?"

There was a big, quick laugh on the other end. "That's just great! Well, how does four-thirty tomorrow morning sound? Give you a half hour to settle in and get gussied up – whatever that process looks like for you. Then another forty-five to prep. We are set up to go live at six. I know it's early on such short notice."

"No," Jade cut him off in her excitement. "It's not early at all. I mean it is," she admitted. "But I love early."

Ethan covered a quick laugh at Jade's excitement, but she didn't even notice.

When she hung up the phone after finalizing a few more details, she froze, looked at Ethan, then shot up.

"I have to go," Jade said.

Ethan panicked. "What?" he asked, worried.

Jade tilted her head at his response. "To bed. I have to go to bed."

"Ha, oh, right. To bed. Of course."

"Okay." Jade threw her hands in the air. "I get to work tomorrow."

She twirled in a circle, stopped and looked at Ethan, laughed at the joy she was feeling, then ran out of the room.

Ethan looked around, suddenly alone. "Okay," he said comically as if Jade hadn't just left him by himself in the den. "No problem. You go. I'll just," he motioned to the TV that resembled giant square cinder blocks, "do this by myself. No, no. I'll be fine."

"I knew you would be."

Jade watched Ethan jump at hearing her voice behind him. She bent down, gave his cheek a quick, happy kiss, then she was gone again.

Ethan blinked, stared, then let his hand come up to his face where Jade had just left him the best goodnight kiss he'd ever had.

CHAPTER 25

Ethan woke up at three just to make sure he had enough time. He didn't know how long it would take Jade to get ready, but he was going to make sure he gave her a proper send-off.

He turned on all of the Christmas lights, then started googling. As the results from his search poured in, he realized he might have overestimated his abilities in the kitchen. But how hard could one of those fancy drinks *really* be?

While he waited for three different kinds of chocolate to melt, he flipped on the TV and tuned it in to the local news channel. There was *no way* he was going to miss Jade's newscast.

After getting sucked into an early morning infomercial, Ethan did a quick check of the time and saw it was only three-ten. Jade would probably leave around four to give herself the extra fifteen minutes. So, he had twenty minutes to make the perfect cup.

Before long, the kitchen counter was lined with six paper cups. Each cup held a different amount or different type of chocolate in it.

Ethan leaned down so he was eye-level with the cups, then started talking to them. "Okay, guys. I'm going to add peppermint to each one of you. I don't know how much, and I don't know how little." Ethan thought about what he'd just said and shook his head. "You get what I mean. But," Ethan straightened and marched along the line at they stood at his attention, "I expect at least one of you to be the best tasting peppermint mocha latte Jade Conner has ever tasted."

Ethan stopped, performed an about-face, and looked down at the cups. "Do you understand?"

When there was nothing but silence, Ethan shrugged. It was the season for miracles, but a cup talking back to him might be one miracle he could do without.

So, Ethan turned toward the French press that he'd prepped with the first batch of freshly ground espresso and covered it with piping hot water. Then he waited.

After repeating the brewing process six times, he filled six cups with the espresso and stovetop steamed milk, placed a cap on each one, then stepped back to assess his work.

Then, he wondered, how exactly he was going to find out which recipe tasted the best?

Ethan darted his eyes around the room and locked himself into a stare with a nutcracker posted up in the kitchen. "What?" he asked the white-bearded wooden man. "It's not like she's going to *know* I tried them."

He looked at the clock once more. Jade would be down any minute.

Ethan quickly jumped to the first cup in line and took a sip.

He stood, considered, and said, "Wow, that's good." He held out the cup to look at it, wondering how it's taking him this long to try a peppermint latte.

Ethan moved to the next, then the next, and the next, until he'd sampled each cup.

After testing them all, he crossed his arms as he looked back and said, "Definitely number four."

"Are you talking to your coffee? Or coffee cups? It smells like coffee." Jade tentatively moved into the room and looked around. Then she gave Ethan a skeptical look and asked, "Why are you up?"

Ethan didn't know if it was the excitement of doing something he hoped Jade would like or the six sips of espresso were already kicking in.

"There were a lot of questions in there. I'll try and answer all of them." Ethan moved to Jade, picked up her hand with his, and led her to the island. "Yes, I was talking to the coffee. But they aren't mine. They're yours. Though," he thought about it, "I suppose I'll have one or two unless you want six lattes today."

Ethan took a breath. As Jade peeked at the TV that had already been turned on, he said, "I'm up because I wanted to be up when you left. And I wanted to make you your favorite latte before work. Suddenly it all seems like a little much. Unless you like it." Ethan spied on Jade out of the corner of his eye. "Do you like it?"

Jade squeezed Ethan's hand a little tighter. "I love it." Then she looked at him. "I love it so much."

Ethan nodded. "Then, I definitely recommend numbers four and five."

Jade let his hand go to grab one of the cups. "Well, here I go."

Ethan thought she seemed nervous. But, just the right amount. He smiled. "Hey, break a leg."

"Thanks," Jade said. She started to turn, but she stopped. "Were you watching infomercials this morning? They're terrible."

Ethan shoved his hands in his sweatpants pockets. "I almost bought us protein shakes and a toaster oven."

Jade grinned. "Must not have been too terrible then. Thanks again."

Ethan watched Jade linger for a second longer than she usually would have. Then, taking a chance, he leaned in and placed a tender kiss on the side of her cheek.

Ever since the night before when she'd touched her lips to his face, he couldn't get his mind off of it. And now that he repaid the favor, he wished it would have been her lips.

Jade brought her hand to the side of her face and closed her eyes for the briefest of moments.

Ethan wanted her to stay, but he knew she couldn't. He wished he could have said anything other than what he had to. "You should go."

Jade smiled, nodded, and started out. She looked back once – so happy and so filled with love – then she walked out of sight.

The popcorn was probably overkill. But in Ethan's opinion, this was the television event of the year. Jade was about to read the local station's morning news to the great people of north-central Minnesota. And, after he sampled the first salty bite, he realized popcorn and a peppermint mocha latte were a match made in heaven. He had a feeling there might be a lot more lattes in his future.

Right now, though, he was about to see Jade, and *she* was something he couldn't let his mind linger over when it came to his future.

Ethan licked the salt off of his fingers, took a big glug of a second peppermint latte, then set it down so he could rub the sweaty nerves from his hands.

Right on time, the introduction music started.

This was it!

Ethan scooted forward to sit on the edge of the couch and clicked the volume up on the remote. He didn't want to miss a word.

And there she was.

Jade looked beautiful, natural. Like she was meant to be sitting right where she was. Her laugh was perfect, her voice was happy. She led with a happy winter miracle that happened overnight – Emily Anders welcomed a precious baby girl. And, throughout the hour, she expertly added her own candid commentary to the segments.

Jade was away for a half-hour while the national news cut in – just enough time for Ethan to cook up a pan of bacon and scramble some eggs. Then she was back for another hour, and it was even better than the last.

Ethan blinked at the TV as Jade wished the viewers a magical winter day, and then she was gone.

He pressed the power button on the remote and let silence fill the living room as he tried to process what he'd just seen. Then, like he would have done for his favorite hockey team, Ethan stood and threw his fists in the air and cheered for Jade.

Jade was used to starting her day at four in the morning. What she *wasn't* used to was a day filled with meetings, on-location shoots, and learning everything she needed to know about the area for ten hours straight.

By the time she got home, she stood outside of the door and rested her head against it. She wondered, if not for the freezing cold sensation on her forehead, could she fall asleep right where she stood?

But at the sound of the door latch clicking, Jade's eyes flew open. Her eyes were quick to react, but her angled body wasn't so lucky.

Just as Ethan pulled the door open and started to ask if she was outside, Jade screamed her way into the open space.

Luckily, she crashed into Ethan rather than the floor and sent them both barreling to the ground.

At the sound of the thud they made when they hit the floor – and the grunt that was forced out of Ethan – Jade let out a pleasantly surprised laugh.

"That wasn't nearly as bad as I thought it was going to be," Jade said, sounding weary but happy.

Ethan gasped and struggled out his words. "Speak for yourself."

"Oh! Sorry." Jade rolled off of him, so they were both lying flat on their backs as snow whipped into the room through the open door.

They turned their heads toward each other and grinned as snowflakes landed on their faces.

"Were you sleeping outside?" Ethan asked, sounding coy.

"You know," Jade gave a slight nod, "I thought about it."

"You had a long day."

Jade yawned, then let a huge smile take over her face. "It was the *best* day."

"And you're ready to do it all again tomorrow?"

"More than. Just so long as I find my bed, like, right now."

"How about you eat the chicken that's warming in the kitchen first? I'll serve you in the den, and I'll read you the terms I set forth when I accepted a new *temporary* position at the lumber yard today?"

Jade shot up. "You took it?"

Ethan pulled himself up and wrapped his arms around his knees. He bobbed his head and repeated her words. "I took it."

"I'm so happy for you. How exciting. I should be making dinner for you to celebrate."

"*You* didn't have three hours to kill before you got ready for work this morning. Did you know you can make practically anything in a crockpot?"

Jade lifted a single eyebrow and nudged Ethan with her elbow. "A crockpot. That's very domestic of you."

"If you think that's domestic, I'm not going to tell you what else I did today."

"Ooh, I'm intrigued. Perhaps you can tell me about it over dinner in the den?"

"See you back down here in ten?"

"It's a date."

Jade didn't realize what she said until it was too late. So, rather than sit in awkward silence, she quickly jumped up, like she was on a mission to clean up and change.

Normally, he wouldn't have thought the immediate departure from a woman he was trying to impress was a good thing. But when the ever-confident Jade Conner scrambled away from you after calling your evening together *a date,* it was enough to satisfy any man.

Ethan stood, closed the front door, and wandered to the kitchen. He grinned at how tired but exhilarated Jade had seemed from her day. He wished he could do more for her than throw some chicken and rice in a bowl and serve it to her. There had to be more.

In the kitchen, Ethan used a Christmas mug to scoop rice into a dish, and with the same fork he set out for Jade to use, he stabbed a couple pieces of chicken and plopped them on top. Feeling like it was his first time in a kitchen, he scrambled around looking for a wine glass. With every movement, he became more frustrated.

He knew what he could do – what he *should* do – if he wanted to help Jade. Because there was only one thing she wanted. And after seeing her on the TV screen today, he knew she was meant for more.

Ethan hung his head and used his hands against the island to hold his body up. He didn't have long, so if he wanted to do something for her, he had to do it now.

Slapping the counter, Ethan straightened and pulled out his phone.

His fingers moved quickly as they searched for *Cities One* and navigated to their *Contact* page.

He typed the message quickly – that part wasn't hard. Everything he mentioned in the contact form was true. But, his finger hovered over the *Submit* button, unwilling to press down because he also knew another truth: If he hit send, Jade would be out of his life forever.

Ethan closed his eyes with his finger still in place.

"I can't wait to hear what the guys at the yard said when you accepted."

As Jade walked into the kitchen, Ethan fumbled with his phone at the surprise, and as he caught it, his thumb came down on the button. His eyes flared at what he'd just done. But he clicked the phone closed and shoved it in his pocket, then tried to act cool and natural.

But, he forgot that *nothing* about him was cool or natural. He was icy around the edges, burly on top, and the main staple of his wardrobe was flannel. He was practically Paul Bunyan.

"Are you okay?" Jade asked, clearly giving him the once-over.

"Yeah," Ethan brushed off her concern with an overly casual laugh.

"Because you look a little," Jade paused as she searched for the right word. "Sweaty? Pliable?"

"Pliable? Really?" Ethan asked, wondering what exactly he looked like.

"You know." Jade wiggled her arms and legs to make them look like rubber bands. "Like Gumby."

Jade's eyes grew with humor. "Oh my gosh. Are you trying to *be cool?"*

"Okay, listen, Snow Queen, I don't have to *try* to be anything. I am...okay, probably not cool. But I'm also not *not* cool. So," Ethan stood defensively, then pointed down to the bowl he filled with Jade's dinner. "Can we just go to the den so I can watch you eat?"

Jade pinched her lips together and grinned through a nod.

Without a word, Ethan watched Jade turn, and he swore he saw the hint of a smile on her way into the den.

They talked and laughed, and she ate. Everything felt fun and natural. More than once, Ethan realized he didn't want the evening to end. But, for Jade, it was getting late. And though he could keep sitting there with her, with only the glow of the fire and the Christmas tree lighting their conversation, he knew he had to let her get up to bed.

Ethan finally, and a bit regretfully, said, "I know you have an early morning. I understand if you want to call it a night." He watched her pause, but in the end, Jade reluctantly agreed.

Jade stood slowly and pulled her glass of eggnog close to her body. She turned once to offer him a heartfelt thanks for all that he did for her that day. But then she turned again at his voice.

"Hey," Ethan said, waiting for Jade to turn around. "For what it's worth, the woman I saw today on the news, she was perfect. I'd wake up every morning for the rest of my life to watch her."

CHAPTER 26

Christmas was only one week away, and Jade and Ethan were reveling in the winter beauty, the happy decorations that touched every inch of their respective grandparents' home, and the exhaustion their new lives had brought them.

They started sharing hot chocolate in the evening. Then, rather than retreat to their rooms after dinner, they stayed and put puzzles together or made a Christmas cookie or dessert for sharing.

With the fire blazing and crackling, Ethan read the final page of *A Christmas Carol* and closed the book.

Jade smiled and let the joyful, happy words sink in. She closed her eyes and wished she could live a night like this one over and over again. There wasn't anything out of the ordinary about the day, aside from the time of year. Both she and Ethan had come downstairs around the same time, shared lattes, and then they both headed off to work. After long days of hard but different work, they reunited to share the details over dinner before retreating to the den.

Sipping her hot chocolate, Jade looked at the tree and wondered if this is what it would be like if she and Ethan had been required to come together in the spring, or perhaps the fall? Would a part of her still long for more? Would she still wish that their time together could be extended – or never end?

Or, Jade wondered, did the magic of Christmas have something to do with it? Would Christmas end, and both she and Ethan turn back into two people who hated the idea of having to stay together?

All of the questions in Jade's mind had her thinking about the letters.

"You should spit out some of what's in that head of yours."

Jade's lip curved when she looked at him. "How exactly do you know that anything is going on in my head?"

"You get this furrowed-eyebrow, faraway look in your eyes. It's actually pretty scary. Seems like there's a blizzard going on in there. So, spit it out."

"I have something to show you. Do you want to put your popcorn-making skills to good use?"

Ethan pushed up from his chair. "As a matter of fact, I do. Meet back in ten?"

Jade tried not to let the eager, completely adorable smile Ethan flashed affect her. But it was getting harder not to be affected with every sweet gesture, innocent act of kindness, or most tender of moments that just seemed to happen out of nowhere with him.

Jade nodded. "Perfect."

She waited for him to leave the den before taking a breath to try and calm her nerves. Until just now, she wasn't sure if she was actually going to share the letters with Ethan. But something in the way they had spent the last weeks together reminded her of her grandma and Lenny.

And maybe Ethan would take comfort in knowing more about her grandma just as she had in learning about Lenny.

Hours later, the letters were scattered on the floor in front of the fire. The candles they had lit were burned down into pools of pine-scented wax. And Ethan and Jade were both sitting in the mess as they read letter after letter.

Ethan couldn't believe it. It all made so much sense. And selfishly, he was overwhelmed with more emotion than he knew he had when it came to his grandfather. He had just read through his grandpa's entire life through the letters he had written to his lover, friend, and confidant. And after so much time – so many years – the woman, it seemed, he was always meant to be with.

"Are you okay?" Jade asked.

Ethan held a letter in his hand and looked at the scattered words of life and love all around him. He had no idea what to say or what to think.

"It's just," Ethan started, as he lifted the letters and dropped them down again, "I kind of always felt like I never really knew him. But I did."

Jade felt worried. "I'm sorry, I didn't mean to–"

"No," Ethan stopped her and rephrased his feelings. "No, not like that. I'm grateful. It doesn't make me feel like I didn't know him. I feel like these letters, getting to read his words, his thoughts…it makes me feel like I really *did*. It doesn't surprise me. He actually *was* just like this. I just didn't know the details, that's all."

Jade relaxed and settled in to wait for Ethan to tell her yet another story about Lenny.

"He was happy. No, actually, he was downright jolly."

Jade gave a genuine laugh.

"He," Ethan started, looking down and growing serious. "He loved." Ethan looked back up. "That's it. He just did everything in love."

Jade watched as Ethan scrambled from letter to letter to help tell his story. Finally, he reached for a letter and held it up.

"This one. Grandpa learned Helen was getting married. It's obvious he still loved her more than anything, but rather than be upset or angry, he wished her happiness. He loved her so much he wanted her to be happy in this life, with or without him. Or this one." Ethan held up another. "He kept her friendship and found a new friend in your grandpa as well. He told them both about the lumber company, his marriage to my grandma. He talked about us, about our parents. They shared everything."

"It was lovely." Jade's hands grazed the edges of a letter. "They did. They shared everything. Happiness, good times, funny moments."

"And sad ones."

Jade listened to Ethan say the words she didn't know if she'd be able to speak out loud. She gave a small smile and a matching nod. "They shared the loss of their loved ones together."

"But," Ethan picked up the last they'd pulled out of Jade's box, "in the end, they found each other again."

Ethan handed Jade the letter, and she read it once more.

December 24, 1999

My Love,

It has been so long since I've said those words. My Love.

I am writing to tell you that for me, enough time has passed. I have loved a beautiful wife, had children I'm proud of, and grandchildren that fill me with so much joy. But the vivid memory of this young girl has always had my heart.

I'll wait for you as long as it takes. Even if that means in another lifetime.

Always Yours,

Lenny Brock

Jade noticed Ethan hadn't handed her the picture that had been placed in the letter. When she looked up, he was studying it just as she had studied it night after night when they'd read the letter together for the first time. She didn't need it now; she had memorized the look on her young grandmother's face. The way her smile was laughing at the camera next to a handsome youthful Lenny Brock.

"It had to have been taken before he left for the war."

Jade moved her eyes to Ethan, who was still staring at the picture.

"Look at them holding hands. I think my grandpa is actually laughing. And," Ethan moved the picture closer to the illuminated Christmas tree for better light. "Did you notice the locket your grandma is wearing?"

Ethan handed the picture over to Jade. She took it and looked closely at the necklace she'd noticed draped around her grandma's neck. Jade had wondered about it. She'd even seen her grandma wear it the one time she'd visited.

Jade softened and handed the picture back to Ethan. "I saw her wear it once. The only time I stayed with her here, in this house.

Ethan looked at Jade. He was looking so intimately his stare caused her to blush. Rather than sit with the warmth he was causing in her, she asked bashfully with a hint of laughter, "What?"

"You look like her."

The comment took Jade by surprise. She didn't realize how much hearing that would have her heart soaring. But, that it came from Ethan, that he would notice that detail, had her tipping over the edge.

She could try and convince herself that she hadn't, but she had fallen for Ethan Brock.

CHAPTER 27

It was three days until Christmas, and the house was almost ready. The tables and chairs had been hauled up from storage and draped with crisp linens. The tabletops had been decorated with miniature woodland trees and small brass reindeer. And candles that smelled like Christmas cheer were placed throughout the house.

"I think we're ready," Jade said as they stood in the kitchen looking at what they had initially thought was the world's longest Christmas to-do list.

"I *never* thought I would say this, but I'm excited."

Jade turned to Ethan and grinned. "Yeah," she said. "Me too."

Just as Ethan linked his hand with Jade's, her phone started to ring.

She laughed and rolled her eyes at the timing. "It could be the station. I should take it."

Ethan nodded to the door and gave her a look that said *scram.*

"Hello," Jade answered the phone, still laughing at Ethan's mannerisms.

"Hello, Jade?"

"Yes, this is her," Jade responded professionally, but the moment she heard the voice on the other end of the line, she knew who it was.

"Jade, this is Melissa at Cities One. I'm sorry to intrude on your holiday, but I'm hoping you have a moment."

Jade slid into the den and stood next to the fireplace. "I do."

"Great. I'm just going to jump right in. Jade, we feel we've made a mistake."

"About what?" Jade asked, not understanding the nature of the call or the statement.

"In letting you go. I received notice you were filling in at a smaller station in northern Minnesota. I've tuned in a couple of times, and I have to say, whatever you've found is exactly what we're looking for. Jade?"

Jade couldn't believe what she was hearing. "Yes?"

"We'd like you to come back to Cities One. We'd like you to join our newest anchor in our evening slot."

"You what? I mean, I'm sorry, I don't understand."

"Yes. I can see how this might appear, but Jade, I've watched you the past couple of days," Melissa repeated. "And you are authentic, enthusiastic, direct, and you have found that lightness we were looking for. I have to admit, whatever you've found to cause this shift in you, it's paying off. So, what do you say? Ready to come back in the new year?"

"Um, I guess I'd like a day or two to think about it."

"Of course, just don't wait too long. We've got a show to run."

"Melissa?" Jade asked before her former boss could sign off the call. "How did you hear about my new job?"

"Oh, ah – it was a note that came through our contact page. From a..."

Jade heard Melissa clicking through files on her computer. "Oh, here it is. A contact form submission from an Ethan Brock. I have to say, we owe a lot to Ethan. Now, Jade, I hope to hear from you soon. And, have a Merry Christmas."

Jade brought the phone away from her ear before Melissa had finished talking.

Ethan had reached out to them?

The initial pain that coursed through her body had her bending over. Was Ethan trying to send her away? Why?

Jade stood and took a heavy, tear-filled breath, then looked down at her hand. A hand that only moments earlier he had linked his fingers with.

Ethan wondered what had changed in Jade. She had retreated to her bedroom for the rest of the afternoon, and when she came down for dinner, her conversation was sparse. She only spoke when she was asked a question or was forced to make a plan for the next two days.

Suddenly she seemed tired. Like all of the early mornings were catching up to her. Maybe she just needed a break.

"Tell you what," Ethan said, trying to sound upbeat. "What if we head to the den early tonight? We can do a little reading, then we can both head up and get a good night's sleep?"

Jade gave a half-smile and nodded. "Sure, that sounds good. I am feeling tired. I should let you know that tomorrow is my last day at the station. Then maybe we can begin discussing how we want to handle all of the post-Christmas details."

"Post-Christmas details?" Ethan asked, feeling concerned.

"Yes," Jade said, all at once a stoic, un-emotional professional. Speaking like they were having a business meeting rather than sharing an intimate dinner together.

"We should discuss the details of how we want to list the property and subdivide the land. Perhaps we should offer the house to a member of your family first since they might find it ideal. Especially with the lumber yard so close. Or, you could just buy out my half."

The entire conversation had turned down a road Ethan hadn't even considered going down since the first time they talked about it. In fact, he had it in his mind they wouldn't even have to sell.

Apparently, he was wrong.

And how wrong he had been to think that he and Jade could live here together. Ethan huffed out a laugh at his thoughts. That he thought she might love him and stay.

Ridiculous.

Then he looked up, matching her poise. "Sure, we can talk tomorrow." Ethan pushed up from the table. How foolish he'd been.

Jade wasn't falling in love with him. They were simply getting carried away in somebody else's love story.

CHAPTER 28

Jade walked out of the world's tiniest but most Christmas-y news station she'd ever seen. Even in her heartbreak, she had to admit, the town still pulled at her. Every time she passed a lamppost wrapped in garland, or a tree sparkling with lights, she couldn't help but smile. She loved it here.

"Hey, I'm trying to talk to you."

Jade blinked back to her conversation with Deni, who had called just as she was wrapping up for the day.

"Sorry, Deni. I have so much on my mind right now. Namely, the Christmas party. I'm *so* excited to see you."

Jade heard Deni's smile in her words.

"Me too. I can't wait to see the house. But what else is on your mind?"

In the modest lobby, Jade waved to a couple of new friends who worked at the station before pushing through the door to walk out. But before she made it out, she was stopped by a voice coming from behind her.

"Hey, Jade! Do you have a minute?"

Jade turned to see Ken Marsh sticking his head out of his office. She smiled at him, held up one finger, then mouthed that she'd be over in a minute. And she couldn't help but laugh at the dorky thumbs-up he gave before disappearing.

Yeah, she was definitely going to miss it here.

"Hey Deni, I'm getting called away. Can't wait for Christmas. Love you."

"Love you, too. See you tomorrow!"

From the door where she was standing, Jade was able to take in the entire news station and offices. It was so far from where she thought she would end up, but within days it had become home. She touched the corkboard on the wall to her right that had wrinkled Christmas cards hanging open and smiled at the idea that she could call this her new dream. Maybe she'd apply for a new job outside of the cities. Something like this – at a place just like this.

Jade straightened her jacket, then moved toward Ken's office.

"Jade, come on in. Great show today. Do you have a minute to talk?"

Ethan had never given much thought to working on Christmas Eve. Of course, he'd also never worked, so it hadn't ever been an issue.

But, after only one day of experience, Ethan decided, with all of the treats, cards, and general happiness in all of his new coworkers at the lumberyard, it really wasn't such a bad gig.

They'd work until noon, then they'd all take off early to get home to spend the holidays with their families. And *he* would get home to prepare Christmas Eve dinner with Jade.

After Jade's abrupt departure from dinner the night before, he hadn't been able to sleep. But he decided he wasn't going to go down without a bit of a fight. If she hadn't noticed he'd fallen in love with her yet, he figured he had one more day to help her figure it out.

Lucky for him, as he dug his way through the reading materials left for him, Ethan was given the perfect opportunity to do just that.

So, he'd head out at noon, prep a Christmas Eve dinner that he would share with Jade, and he'd give her the Christmas gift he'd found.

It wasn't a bad plan.

By the time he finally. got home, Ethan had four hours to get dinner prepared, roasted, and on the table. He had bought a small chicken, winter vegetables, stuffing, and boxed mashed potatoes. He figured if he was going all out on the chicken, she'd hardly notice that the potatoes started out as a bunch of flakes.

While the chicken roasted, Ethan showered, dressed in a new sweater, and trimmed his beard. And he didn't look half bad if he did say so himself.

Ethan didn't know when to expect Jade, but when he heard the door click and creak open at four, he froze. Then when he heard the footsteps, he knew he'd be caught in the act.

Jade peeked her head around the corner to the kitchen. "Wow." It was all she said as she took in the chaotic sight and the delicious smell.

Ethan gave her a questioning look. "*Wow* to this?" He pointed to himself, grinning. "Or, *wow* to this?" He pointed next to the stove, then circled his finger around to the kitchen island that probably looked more like a war zone.

"Can I answer yes to both?"

"You can."

"I have to say, I've seen that apron before, but never has it seemed so *small*."

"Festive?" Ethan offered his word at the same time as Jade.

When she laughed, his heart filled with so much hope and joy. He just hoped it wasn't all for nothing.

"Yes, sorry. Definitely festive. But really, it smells so good in here. Is that stuffing?" Jade moved farther into the kitchen to try and spy on the contents of the oven.

"It might be, but you can't look. *If* you'd like to join me for a highly anticipated Christmas Eve dinner, I would ask you to meet me back here at five."

Ethan watched Jade flick a pretty eyebrow up, but it didn't ease his nerves; he was still holding his breath.

"Christmas Eve dinner sounds lovely."

It didn't take Jade long to change into a sweater that looked jolly enough to match Ethan's. She didn't miss the detail of his nice wardrobe that was hidden under her grandma's old apron. And she definitely didn't miss that he'd trimmed his beard for the event.

So really, how could she say no to all of that? Well, all of that *and* the heavenly smell that pulled her into the kitchen in the first place.

Even though she was dressed and presentable, Jade wasn't ready to go down just yet. Instead, she'd let Ethan finish what he'd set out to do, and she'd take some time alone.

She read through her grandma's letters once more, sat next to the Christmas tree, and finally when it was time to head down, she did. There was no harm in spending a nice Christmas Eve with Ethan. They might head their separate ways after Christmas, but it didn't take away the fact that Ethan was a different man than she thought he was. It didn't make the love and affection she found for him any less.

So, spending Christmas Eve alone with him would be lovely. In fact, she'd savor it. She'd try and take in every moment so she could remember it forever.

As Jade turned toward the kitchen for the second time that night, the room looked entirely different. The kitchenette table was set for two. A wine bottle sat in the middle, and Christmas place settings marked each of their spots.

The lights were off, but candles were glowing, Christmas trees were lit, and every tiny house, trinket, and light-up decoration had come to life.

"What do you think?" Ethan asked as she stepped into the room.

It was all Jade could do to keep from crying at the beauty and the sentiment.

"It's perfect," she finally whispered. And it was.

As she moved closer to the table, she noticed a small wrapped box sitting on one of the Christmas plates.

Ethan came up behind the chair and pulled it out. "Allow me."

Jade smiled, gently touched his cheek, then slid into the chair.

"I was going to wait until after dinner, but I don't think I'll make it that long. I want to give you your gift before Christmas. Open it."

Ethan sat across from Jade as she eyed him, then gracefully picked up the small box. She pulled the ribbon and set it aside. Then she lifted the top.

Jade's eyes welled immediately. When she realized what it was, she looked up at Ethan, who was smiling bigger than she'd ever seen.

"It belongs to you."

He meant it. From the moment he realized it was Helen's locket that had been left for him in the box of Christmas books, there wasn't any doubt that it belonged to Jade.

Jade looked down again and couldn't believe it. Her grandma's locket shined up at her, reflecting every intimate light sparkling around her.

She wanted to tell him how she felt. To say to him that even before the locket, she had fallen in love with him.

But knowing their time was at its end, she held the words in.

Jade pressed the locket to her heart and closed her eyes. When she opened them again, she looked at Ethan and whispered, "Thank you. Thank you so much."

CHAPTER 29

It was Christmas morning, and Jade knew this would be her only bit of quiet alone time she'd have all day. So, she cherished it.

Upon waking early, Jade had crept out of bed to turn on the Christmas tree lights and the ones draped on her bedposts. Then she jumped back into the warmth of her bed so she could enjoy them.

After a while, she rose and put on activewear that she knew would get her through all of the running around and prep work for the party. But as casual and comfortable as she wanted to be, she couldn't wait to put on her grandmother's locket.

Jade connected the clasp behind her head, then leaned in close to the mirror so she could admire it. The intricate design looked like a snowflake.

For a moment, Jade wrapped it in her hands, held it close to her chest, and closed her eyes. But, as a thought crossed her mind, she opened her eyes and considered the locket.

She turned it once and found the edge. Jade slid her thumbnail into the slit on the side, and the locket popped open.

Happy tears found her eyes as she looked at the engraving.

"My love," Jade whispered the words scrawled on the inside.

"After all that time," Jade said to herself and to her grandma. "I'm so grateful for our family. But," Jade paused so she could hold the locket close once more, "I'm so happy you found your way back to Lenny."

A tear slipped out of the corner of Jade's eye. She wiped it and let her head fall just a bit but lifted it high as she said the words she didn't realize she needed to say until now. "Grandma, I'm so sorry. I love you so much. I always have."

Jade was startled at the knock on her bedroom door. She gave one last squeeze to her locket before letting it rest lightly against her chest, then moved to the door. When she opened it, she saw Ethan standing on the other side, in candy cane socks and a matching shirt.

Jade snorted out a laugh. "What are you wearing?"

"What do you mean *what am I wearing?* I'm wearing the only attire that should be acceptable on Christmas Day." Ethan wobbled his head back and forth. "At least until the people come."

"The guests?" Jade suggested.

"Sure," Ethan agreed. "Though, my dad can get a little unruly. I only invited him because I had to."

Jade knew there was a bit of truth hiding in Ethan's joke, but she had a feeling things would start to shift between him and his father after these past several weeks.

"Anyway, are you ready to come downstairs in a couple minutes to get started?"

Jade shrugged and said, "I'm ready now."

Ethan furrowed his eyebrows. "No, you're not. You haven't changed into your outfit yet."

Jade eyed Ethan, suspecting what he had up his sleeve. "You didn't."

As Ethan pulled a matching candy cane outfit out from behind him, Jade laughed. "This is ridiculous, you know that, right?"

Ethan shrugged. "One woman's ridiculous is another man's fun. Let's start the day with peppermint lattes and presents!"

Jade's eyes widened with dread. "Presents?" she asked, worried that she hadn't gotten Ethan more than a Christmas ornament so they could remember this holiday together.

"Oh yeah. I think you're going to love it. You change. I'm going down. Hurry!"

Jade stared at the red and white stripes in her hands and wondered if maybe she hadn't put enough thought into Christmas. But, when had there time to think about more than the party? Besides, when she wasn't thinking about the Christmas party, she was busy convincing herself to forget about Ethan. That included ignoring any urges to get him Christmas presents.

Jade changed and walked to the kitchen. When she didn't see Ethan, she walked all the way in and circled the island. Then she wandered to the front of the house and tried the library, and when she didn't find him there, she moved into the den.

"Merry Christmas!" Ethan was standing in a Santa Claus hat next to a small table set for two.

Jade hadn't had this feeling in so long. The excitement and anticipation of the day ahead suddenly rushed into her. Ethan had lit the fire and turned the Christmas tree lights on. The table had the pretty Christmas dishes set on it, and their peppermint lattes were in mugs that looked like snowmen.

Jade laughed. "Merry Christmas, Ethan."

She moved to the table and her eyes danced with happiness. "My present, I assume?"

"Two, extra gooey, caramelly, and delicious Christmas caramel rolls. Both for you."

"You didn't get one?"

Ethan smiled and shook his head. "No, my Christmas present this year was getting to spend the holiday with you."

"Ethan," Jade began, but he held up his hands.

"No," he said. "It was my present. You aren't allowed to say anything."

Jade grinned. "Well, in that case, all I'll say is, there's nobody I'd rather spend this Christmas with than you."

If Christmas morning was the picture-perfect snow globe setting for Jade and Ethan, then the afternoon of setting up and getting ready for the evening party was like somebody took the jolly snow globe and shook it nonstop for hours.

After breakfast, mid-morning was filled with finishing the food, setting out the gifts, prepping the bar, and setting the mood with Christmas music. As they darted back and forth between rooms, every once in a while, their paths crossed. When they did, Ethan would take Jade's hand and spin her around as they ran by each other. Then they'd laugh through their exhaustion and keep going.

Then, finally, they had done it.

Jade retreated to her room to clean up and change into a Christmas dress. It was a family tradition to wear your best on the most wonderful day of the year. And by the time she walked out, friends and family had already started to arrive.

They greeted friends and relatives into the home they'd decorated for Christmas. They ushered and served as if it was their own. They laughed and told stories of when they arrived, and how somewhere during the holidays, the magic had them winning each other over and getting along after all.

Deni, of course, was insufferable. She didn't let Jade forget that she had feelings for Ethan the entire night. From the moment they wrapped each other in a big hug when Deni walked in, straight through until they walked up the stairs together to end the night.

Jade was grateful for the space Ethan was giving her to be with her family on Christmas night. And with Deni in particular. She hadn't realized how much she missed her sister – or her sister's banter.

"Have you told him how you feel?" Deni asked the moment they stepped into Jade's bedroom.

Jade smiled as she started removing her earrings and unclipping her hair. "No, I can't. We agreed how things would go after the holidays."

"Uh, hello. You love each other. Did you see the way he was looking at you tonight? Like, all night."

"It's not fair to assume he *loves* me," Jade said.

Deni smirked as she noticed Jade hadn't denied that she loved Ethan. She didn't need to say a word. Jade read her sister's smug face like an old favorite book.

"Yes, I love him," she responded to Deni's expression. "I was so wrong about him. And about grandma." Jade looked down as she leaned into the doorframe of the bathroom. She shrugged. "And, he helped me realize that."

"Oh my gosh, would you stay here?" Deni suddenly asked as she realized the seriousness of her sister's feelings.

Jade smiled and said, "I have something to tell you."

After most of their guests had gone, Ethan had wished Jade a Merry Christmas, then watched her retreat to her bedroom with Deni. What he would have given to follow her.

Ethan dropped his head. He knew what he would have given – everything. But he wouldn't risk her happiness. And to tell her that he loved her meant doing just that.

He didn't want to give her a reason to pass up the opportunity she'd been given. Not everybody got a second chance, but Jade had. And she deserved it. What she didn't deserve was him throwing a wrench into her well-crafted career plan.

Ethan pushed off the steps he'd found himself sitting on and decided to move into the den. He'd grown to love the den. It had become Jade's and his place of comfort. Where they went to share stories about their day, where they went to relax, and where he had grown to love her.

As he turned the corner into the room, Ethan realized he wasn't going to be alone.

"Ethan," Jeremy Brock said as he looked up from the fire he'd been standing next to when he heard his son walk into the room.

"Dad, hi. Ah, sorry, I thought I'd be alone in here. Are you and mom staying the night?" Ethan stopped in the doorway.

"Come in, please."

The sound of his dad's voice caught Ethan off-guard. It was tamer than usual. Calm, even.

"Can I pour you a drink?"

"Sure, yeah. That would be great," Ethan said as he moved to meet his dad in front of the bar.

"I don't think we're staying," Jeremy started while he pulled the eggnog out of the fridge. He motioned to it quickly. "Your grandpa did always make the best."

Ethan chuckled and nodded. "He did."

"Ethan?" Jeremy handed the drink to his son and sighed. "Son, I'm sorry."

Ethan shook his head and asked, "For what?"

"I–ah, I shouldn't have pushed you out. I shouldn't have forced you to try and fit into an eight-by-eight-foot box." Jeremy grinned and got the small laugh from Ethan he was looking for. "I got a call from Jeb a couple weeks ago."

Ethan turned serious and looked up.

"He told me that you accepted a temporary job to step in and help them. Before you say anything," Jeremy spoke before Ethan could respond. "I want you to know, hearing that you took that job didn't feel any better than asking you to move out of the cabin. Because when I heard the news, I felt terrible. I worried you'd accepted a position you might have hated just because I had forced you to do it. If working for our family's company isn't something you want to do, I want to encourage you to find something new."

Ethan didn't cry, but the tears had dampened in his eyes just the same.

"I'm proud of you, Ethan. I always have been. I always will be."

That did it. A couple tears trickled out as he first held out his hand to shake his dad's, but he felt them all come down as his dad pulled him in for a hug that was years overdue.

"Thanks, Dad."

"I love you, Ethan. More than you'll ever know. Merry Christmas."

"Merry Christmas." Ethan laughed as he tried to gather himself. Then he joked, "If you tell Mom I cried…"

"Secret's safe with me. Want to sit?" Jeremy offered.

"Yeah. And Dad, I haven't told anybody this yet. But I'm actually going to be replacing Jeb permanently."

"Ethan," Jeremy sounded surprised and worried.

"No, Dad. I really like it. I love being outside. I love working with my hands. And I like the guys. I look forward to it every day."

Jeremy grinned then.

"What?" Ethan asked.

"And what do you look forward to at the end of the day?"

Ethan knew where his dad was going. And like the same conversation he'd been having with himself since the moment he realized he was in love with Jade, talking about it more wasn't going to change the outcome.

"She is the best part of my morning and the reason I go to bed happy at night. She's my Christmas morning – every day."

"Have you told her?" Jeremy wondered aloud.

Ethan shook his head. "She has dreams that don't include me."

Jeremy nodded but not in agreement. It was the gesture of a man who knew more than the one he was talking to. "I'm not going to say more than this, but just remember, love is a dream all its own. And hey, if that fails, don't wait too long. Christmas miracles are only good for another hour or two."

Ethan couldn't help but laugh. "Yeah, thanks, Dad. Really helpful."

"I thought it was pretty good."

Ethan just grinned. "Yeah, it was alright."

When the house was finally dark and the celebration was over, Ethan thought about his dad's words.

Christmas miracles are only good for another hour or two.

He heard Jade and Deni still talking and laughing in Jade's room, and he didn't want to impose, but he needed to make sure he didn't miss out on his miracle.

Ethan hadn't written a single letter in his entire life. He'd written thank you cards under the watchful eye of his mom when he was young, and he'd signed birthday and get-well cards. But he'd never written a letter.

He'd gone through his grandpa's letters in the den once more and realized they had all been written on Christmas Eve. It was his grandpa's tradition. Ethan and Jade might have borrowed each of their grandparents' love stories for a little bit, but he was willing to start their own.

If he learned anything from his grandpa, it was that he could love Jade. And he could do it unconditionally.

He could love her through her joys, through her dreams, through everything life would bring her.

So, with only the glow of the fire and the Christmas tree, Ethan sat down with pen and paper to start his own love story.

Every Christmas, for the rest of his life, Ethan would write Jade a letter.

Because to him, he would always be hers.

CHAPTER 30

This was the one time in Ethan's life that he slept worse the night *after* Christmas than the night before. But, of course, when his mind stopped racing about when and how he would give Jade his first Christmas letter, he finally fell into a hard sleep.

So, instead of catching her early in the morning, he'd walked into her tidy, empty bedroom.

Ethan looked around, feeling like he was invading Jade's privacy, but he wanted to put the letter in just the right place.

First, he set it on the bench at the end of her bed but decided it seemed like he just tossed it there without a thought. Then he tried her pillow but shook his head as he thought that might send the wrong message. Best to leave the bed out of things at this stage in their relationship – the *I wonder if she even loves me* stage, or the *I can't believe I just confessed my love for her* stage.

Ethan swiped at the card and clumsily sent it flying across the room. "Oh, come *on,*" he said as he bent down to see where it went.

Ethan eyed it on the floor on the other side of the bed. And rather than standing, he just stayed on all-fours and crawled his way to the other side.

"Hey. What ya doing?"

Ethan stopped moving and pinched his eyes shut, praying that if he squeezed hard enough, he might disappear. Because if the tone of Deni's voice wasn't embarrassing enough, he was going to have to explain why he was crawling around on Jade's bedroom floor.

After a minute, Ethan tucked his head and opened one eye to see if Deni was still standing in the doorway.

Unfortunately, she hadn't disappeared. And to make matters worse, her smile let Ethan know he probably didn't have to tell her a thing about why he was there.

Jade was right. Deni really did seem to know everything.

Well, rather than avoid it, Ethan finished his crawl to the Christmas letter, picked it up, then stood up and looked at Deni.

"I think you know what I'm doing," Ethan said.

Deni shrugged and folded her hands. "Only if you're sneaking into my sister's room to tell her you love her. If you're not doing that, then no, I don't know what you're doing."

Ethan squinted at Deni. He suddenly understood the irritation and the admiration. What an intriguing combination.

"Right, well. Since we don't have to get into that, is there any way you can tell me where she might have gone this morning?"

Like her answer was the most casual thing she'd ever done in her life, Deni responded as she leaned on the doorframe. "Oh, yeah. She said something about needing to go accept a job. I'm sure she'll be back soon. I'm sure she'll be back in time for your meeting to settle house details."

New job?

Ethan looked down and shook his head. A new job. Of course she would take the job Melissa offered her back at Cities One. It was what she always wanted. And wasn't *he* the one that led her right to it?

"Still with me?" Deni dipped her head a bit, looking less than concerned.

Ethan was sure he looked like he might get sick right there in the middle of the room. But he had to hold it in. He had to be better than that.

Hadn't he, just the night before, accepted the fact that he would love Jade no matter what? That included new jobs. It included her being far away from him. It even included the possibility that she might not love him back.

Ethan nodded. "Thanks, Deni. I'm just going to–" Ethan lifted the letter to show Deni why he was there. He hoped the gesture was enough to earn some alone time.

Deni smiled and nodded. "Any time. And hey, Merry Christmas, Ethan."

"Yeah, you, too, Deni."

When he was alone again, Ethan tapped the letter against his hand and looked around. Then he looked at the Christmas tree. He grinned because he knew the first thing that Jade probably did that morning was flick on the delicate lights that adorned the fragrant branches, then crawl back into bed.

He moved over to it and brushed the branches. Then he looked down when he heard some of the needles softly tap a box lying beneath it. Ethan brushed a few fallen pine needles off the top and looked under the lid.

Jade had placed their grandparent's letters under the tree. Her act and sentiment had Ethan grinning.

"Well," Ethan said to himself. "We've borrowed so much already. What's one more?"

Just like the letters from Christmases past had been placed beneath the tree, Ethan did the same with his. Then he stood and walked out to get ready for what was maybe going to be the most heartbreaking meeting of his life.

CHAPTER 31

At one minute to eleven, Sully and Ethan were awkwardly staring at each other in the library.

"I don't suppose you know where Ms. Ja–"

"No," Ethan responded so quickly that Sully didn't even get to finish his question. "No, I don't know where she is."

Ethan rubbed his hands down his face. He might love her, but that didn't mean she couldn't irritate him. He was growing angrier by the minute. And they only had one more of those left.

Ethan kept one hand over his face to hide the disbelief as the second hand ticked closer to eleven.

"I'm here! Don't start! Sorry. Oh my gosh, I can't believe I made it."

Both Sully and Ethan looked toward the door in time to see Jade burst into the room.

Ethan eyed the unopened letter Jade was holding in her hand and sent her a questioning, but also an accusing, glance.

"Sorry," Jade said in a rush. "I was talking to my realtor."

"Wow, already?" Ethan couldn't resist the flare of temper that passed through him as he put the moments of the morning together. First, she's accepting her new job, then she's talking to realtors to sell off her half of the estate.

Jade tilted her head and gave Ethan a strange look.

Sully's hefty sigh pulled them both out of their moment. "I see we're still fighting. Good to know some things never change. Though I have to admit, you had me going for a minute there. Good on you."

"Yeah, you and me both," Ethan said as he plastered a fake smile on his face. But, what really irritated Ethan, was that even knowing Jade was making plans and moving on, he *still* thought she was beautiful, and he *still* was head over heels in love with her. He supposed that's where most of the agitation was coming from.

Jade eyed Ethan at his comment, then slowly turned her attention to Sully and asked, "Sully, could Ethan and I have a minute alone?"

"Yes," Sully said without hesitation. "I believe I'm going to need a beverage for this. I'll be in the den when you're ready." Sully started walking out but paused in the doorway and shook his head at Jade and Ethan before saying, "Good luck."

Jade smiled a bit at Sully and his evident bewilderment of her and Ethan's relationship. But what she wasn't finding funny was Ethan's sudden irritation with her.

"What's going on with you?" Jade asked.

"You tell me?" Ethan fired back.

Jade paused and figured she might as well tell Ethan her news.

When Jade opened her mouth to speak, Ethan snow plowed forward. "Why are you talking to realtors already? I thought we agreed we would do all of that together?"

"I, ah. I guess I just thought the sooner, the better." Jade shook her head.

"And the job? Were you even going to tell me?" Ethan's arms were outstretched, practically pleading. It wasn't a good look, but this wasn't the time for keeping up his manly image.

At the question, a little twinkle of understanding flickered across Jade's face.

With the realization of where his mood was coming from, she smiled and chose to ignore his question.

After a moment, Jade held up the letter and asked, "What's this?"

"Doesn't matter," Ethan said, not meaning it at all.

"It might. Is it from you?"

"Maybe." Ethan finally found a place for his hands on his hips.

Jade nodded. "Sully, you can come back in now."

Ethan's face shot up from the spot on the floor where he'd been staring to look Jade in the eye. "No, he can't. We're still fighting."

Jade sighed. "We're not fighting."

Ethan stretched out his hands and appeared to be dangling by the end of his rope. Finally, he yelled, "We *are* fighting!"

"I think I'm going to read this." Jade started opening the letter she'd found beneath her Christmas tree as Sully walked back into the room.

"You can't just stop arguing with me to read my Christmas letter."

Sully ducked out of the way so Ethan's words wouldn't pelt him as he walked between them.

Before Jade's eyes hit the paper, she looked up and answered, "I can read a letter from the man I love any time I want to."

Ethan started to yell but tripped over Jade's unexpected words.

Jade used the welcome silence to read Ethan's letter.

She let the love from the letter fill her heart as she read the words he'd written to her on Christmas Day. Then, when she reached the end, tears filled her eyes.

Maybe we can start a love story of our own?

Always Yours, Ethan Brock

Jade silently folded the letter and placed it back into the envelope. Then she turned toward Sully, who had taken his seat behind the desk.

"I would like to keep my half of the estate."

"What?" Ethan jumped in and stood right next to Jade. "How do you plan on doing that with your fancy new job?"

Jade looked at Ethan. "Didn't you hear me tell you that I'm in love with you?"

Jade didn't wait for Ethan to respond. Instead, she just looked back at Sully, who was staring at the two of them like they were crazy.

"I recently accepted a position at the local television station as their lead anchor. And though I don't think it matters much to the terms of the contract, I would like to note that I've fallen in love with Ethan Brock. Therefore, I would like to keep my half of the estate and share it with him – in whole. Or, if he doesn't find those terms suitable, I would like to forfeit my portion of the estate entirely."

Sully opened his mouth to speak, but Ethan cut him off. Neither of them saw Sully drop his face into his hands.

"You took a job here?"

Jade took a step toward Ethan and looked deep into his eyes, searching them, looking for any sign that he might love her back. Then she said, "I did. I don't want to leave this town. I don't want to leave this home. I don't want to leave you."

Ethen let out a breath and brought a hand to Jade's cheek, and she leaned into it. Then she reached for it with her hands and held it as she went on.

"I want to share all of our meals together. I want to decorate not only for Christmas but for every holiday together. I want to go hiking and snowshoeing and take sleigh rides with you. Though," Jade wobbled her head back and forth briefly, "I think we should limit our distance, or we could work in a prize for me at the end of an activity together. Just throwing things out there."

Jade grinned when Ethan laughed.

"I want to bring you lunches at the lumber yard and talk about our days over dinner. And I want to read with you at night – every night. But most of all," Jade said while holding back tears of hope and joy, "I want this." She held up the Christmas letter Ethan had written her.

Then Jade shrugged. "I want our own love story."

Ethan moved in quickly and wrapped Jade up into a hug that sent them spinning.

When they stopped, Ethan held her face, and without a moment's hesitation, he kissed her.

He kissed her with a passion that left no question in her heart or in her mind that Ethan Brock was in love with her, too. But he told her anyway.

Ethan finally pulled back, but only a bit. With his forehead resting on hers, Ethan said, "Jade Conner, I love you. All of you. And I can't wait to start our own love story."

At that moment, Jade felt like she heard angels singing.

Ethan grinned and kissed her once more.

"Ah-hem." Sully cleared his throat to get their attention.

Jade and Ethan turned, still holding each other close. And, if they weren't mistaken, they could have sworn they saw Sully wipe away a tear.

"Sully," Ethan started. "I have also taken a new, permanent position."

Jade gasped and squeezed Ethan. "You did?"

Ethan grinned. "I did." Then he continued to direct his words to Sully. "*We* would like to keep the estate in its entirety. If you feel we've met the prerequisites."

"Well," Sully started. "I think you have...and then some. It's really quite simple from here on out. As the new owners of the Brock Family Trust, you have all you need in this folder." Sully held up a red file folder, then set it down again. "I am here to guide you and answer questions as needed. Oh, and there is one more thing, seeing as you've found yourself in this situation." Sully waved a finger between Jade and Ethan, who were still locked in an embrace. "You also get this."

Sully used an old key to unlock one of the top drawers of the desk.

At his slow, calculated movements, Jade and Ethan stole a questioning glance at each other.

Then, Sully set a small, blue velvet box on the desk in front of Ethan. Then he said, "It was Helen's. Lenny bought it before he was sent off to the war. It took a lifetime, but in the end, he was finally able to give it to her. They requested, in the extenuating circumstance the two of you found yourselves in love, it too fell to your ownership."

Jade brought a hand to her mouth because, without thinking twice, Ethan kept her other hand in his and dropped to his knee.

Ethan smiled and said, "Well, Snow Queen, what do you say? Are you ready to start our own love story?"

At first, Jade could only nod. Between the laughter and the indescribable happiness, she didn't know if she could speak.

"Yes. Yes. My answer will forever be yes."

Ethan swooped her up and danced her in a circle.

When they parted to look at the happiness they shared, Jade said, "I don't know if I've ever had a better Christmas."

"I promise, from this Christmas on, each one will be better than the last."

As they kissed once more, Jade and Ethan felt the magic of the season, and the promise of tomorrow, as they started to write their own Christmas love story.

Merry Christmas!

THANK YOU!

I'm so humbled that you've taken the time to read my book. I can't tell you how much of my heart goes into each and every word.

I WOULD BE SO GRATEFUL FOR YOUR HONEST REVIEW OF:
A Borrowed Christmas Love Story

Click the link, or scan the QR code below to be taken to Amazon.
(Hover your phone over the image!)

LET'S CELEBRATE THE SEASON

Continue on to the next page for a special excerpt of ***The Problem with Love Potions,*** a magical, fall romantic comedy.

Then, check out some of Katie's favorite holiday new releases, and oh so wonderful holiday classics.

Finally, if you're interested in Katie's sweet with heat Taking Chances series, start reading *Becoming Us* for FREE when you subscribe to her newsletter.

A SPECIAL EXCERPT

THE PROBLEM WITH love POTIONS

A LANTERN LANE ROM COM

A ROMANTIC COMEDY

KATIE BACHAND

CHAPTER 1

Alice smiled at poor Blanche. It must be hard to be seventy and still want to date all of the available men at the small-town watering hole. If Alice thought her pool of men was shrinking, the devil only knows what Blanche thought of her own.

But then again, she and everybody else at Witches' Brew, Alice's quaint coffee shop in downtown Lantern Lane, knew precisely what Blanche thought.

"I gave Tom that latte, and he didn't so much as bat an eye at me." Blanche pointed her finger at the board behind Alice that listed all of the *potential* benefits of her beverages. "It says right there it's supposed to enhance one's attraction to another. Now I don't know much about all that scientific mumbo-jumbo, but I think that ingredient there, the one that says *Dehydroepiandrosterone,*" Blanche fumbled through the long, jumbled word, "right next to *testosterone*. I'm pretty sure that means sex!"

Alice didn't have to move her eyes around the room to hear the townspeople's thoughts. She didn't even have to be a witch to guess. But she was a witch, and she could hear their thoughts, so it took an impressive amount of willpower to hold a straight face and address Blanche's concerns.

Alice swiped a stray, fiery red curl off of her forehead and sent a silent little truth spell in Blanche's direction. Nobody noticed the spark that flicked Blanche in the nose or the way she stood a little straighter when the magic took hold.

"Blanche, I am so sorry you feel the *Love and Spice Latte* didn't have the desired effect. But, I wonder, can you tell me that you are absolutely certain that Tom drank the latte you gave him?"

Blanche stared at the ceiling like the previous day's memory was stored in a Rolodex hovering above her.

"You know," Blanche started, "I didn't *see* him drink it. I set it on his desk after I snuck into his office. I didn't want to get caught because that security guard at the front desk of that tiny clinic is a stickler for only letting people in that have an appointment or an illness."

Alice nodded and furrowed her brows, showing Blanche she completely understood and sympathized with her crazy antics. "Yes, I see. I believe you know

Kane is the security guard there," Alice agreed, to keep Blanche talking, but couldn't resist bringing up the fact that everybody knew everybody in their little port town.

"Well, yes. Of course, I know Kane. But it's not like that does me any good. He doesn't give an inch. I try to schmooze my way in, but he's a stickler, I tell you. Anyway, after careful observation," Blanche lowered her tone and leaned in, "I learned that it takes him about 44 seconds to use the restroom. So, naturally, I realized that was my window of opportunity. I had to get in and get out. You know?"

Curious, Alice wondered aloud, "Blanche, did you happen to notice anybody paying unusual attention to you yesterday? Say – oh, I don't know – lingering around you, or hugging you, or complimenting you, or just, well, anything?" Alice bent over the counter and used one arm to hold her head on her fist and the other to casually gesture as she asked the question.

"You know, now that you mention it, Candice did race out of the clinic after me yesterday. Didn't even bother to change out of that god-awful clinic gown they give you. Looks like old sheets. And that terrible way it flaps open in the back – leaves *nothing* to the imagination. Anyway, she just raved over my cooking, and between you and me, I'm not that great of a cook. Then she gave me an unusually long hug before Tom came out and got her. I think she might have sniffed me once or twice, too. Strangest thing. But that really isn't the point here."

Alice heard Blanche speaking, but the air in the room had changed. A fog settled in as if her coffee shop became an open field on a cold, hazy morning. Everybody blurred in the gray. She wondered if the others could see it. But as she looked around the room, they were all going on about their day as if nothing was out of the ordinary.

Alice felt her heart thud against her chest, and when she saw him, it stopped her heart for a split second. Then he disappeared.

"What in the?"

"Alice, are you even listening to me?" Blanche reprimanded Alice for her blank, disinterested look.

Alice blinked twice, and suddenly the room was alive and bustling as it was before she had her vision.

Alice didn't get visions often, but when she did, they meant trouble. Just ask any player on their '03 high school football team. She'd envisioned the star quarterback going down with an injury and the team losing a heartbreaker. Of course, they didn't know she was a witch, but Riley, her cousin and best friend - and sports enthusiast - did. And Riley didn't talk to her for a week after it came true.

"Blanche," Alice started, wondering if she could dig any information out of one of the prominent members of the town rumor-mill, "have you heard anything about a new–"

"Alice! This is serious. I will not be distracted by questions about that new deputy, Sheriff Lane Paxon hired. Can you help me with your faulty drink or not?"

New deputy.

Law enforcement officers were typically an area where witches tended to tread lightly. But at least she got a bit of information.

Alice smiled sweetly. She supposed she could focus on the comical task at hand. Because, poor Blanche, she just needed somebody to love.

"Okay, Blanche," Alice began her instruction as she moved to the right to start making the *Love and Spice Latte*, "this is what I'm going to need you to do: take this latte, go straight up to Tom when he gets off work. Tell him you'd like to share a coffee with him if he has the time. Then walk with him down to the shore, and enjoy the sunset while you sip your drinks. By the time the sun goes down, I can almost guarantee Tom will be smitten."

Blanche looked more than satisfied. Especially when two lattes were handed over, and she learned they were both free of charge. Blanche darted for the door, yelling her *thanks* over her shoulder.

Alice watched Blanche leave and shook her head. Alice knew Blanche was headed straight to the clinic to wait for Tom.

"What'd you put in it?"

Alice turned to see Paige Haskell, her young, quirky, but undeniably beautiful employee, wrapping an apron around her waist to start her shift and grinned.

Paige suspected there was something magical in the beverages they sold, but she had never been able to prove it. And the countless times she asked Alice if she was a witch – as ridiculous as the question sounded – Paige could never tell if Alice was joking or not when she'd reply, *Of course, aren't we all?*

But Paige had made up her own mind. You couldn't be as striking as Alice, have her track record of broken hearts left in her wake, and an insane number of satisfied customers. Her drinks were delicious, but at the end of the day, a good coffee was just a good coffee. There had to be some kind of sorcery or magic at play.

Alice waited for Paige's thoughts to slow. "Nothing out of the ordinary. Just the usual cloves, ginger, nutmeg…times two. Poor Tom isn't going to know what hit him."

Paige rested against the counter and put her hands on her hips. "More like Blanche isn't going to know what hit *her* once Tom kicks in."

Alice touched a finger to the side of her nose and agreed, thinking *you have no idea.*

When the bell on the door chimed, the two women shared a laugh before Alice turned to greet the customer. When she turned, she froze, and all she could say was, "It's you."

CHAPTER 2

Theo Parker was none-the-wiser, but he pulled into Lantern Lane when a stranger named Blanche was talking her way into two free lattes.

As he drove through the dense, tree-laden lane, Theo wondered why on earth the road he drove in on was still gravel. But he had to admit, the bumpy ride and the hazy layer of fog that accompanied it seemed more like an appropriate welcoming party than a nuisance.

He reminded himself he wasn't running. It was just a new experience. A minor, temporary relocation.

Was it his fault his buddy just happened to have an opening at their local Sheriff's Office? No. Was it a blow to his ego to transition from patrolling a massive city to a town of about one thousand? Not at all. Was he still a little bitter about the way his ex-girlfriend had left him for not one but two friends they'd shared since college? Well, possibly. But if anybody asked him, he'd deny it until his face matched his old blue uniform.

"What the–"

Theo's old truck rumbled over what his GPS showed as the final bridge into Lantern Lane. The change in the air was so sudden he stopped his vehicle and stuck his head out of the squeaking crank window. He turned and saw the fog, still thick as mud, huddled over the bridge. Then he sat forward again and stared at so many fall-colored oranges, reds, and yellows he had to blink a couple times to make sure he wasn't dreaming. The stark contrast seemed like he just passed through a portal into another world.

That crisp golden hue that so often accompanied the fall sunlight made everything look mystical. His eyes traveled along the road lined with trees that were still sporting their water-colored leaves. They paused only a time or two to take in the occasional apple tree. Then they finally settled on the tiny port town at the bottom of the hill.

If Theo wasn't so dead-set on sulking and feeling sorry for himself, he would have forced himself to enjoy the view. It might have been a year since his ex left him, but that didn't make the sting any less.

As he pressed his foot against the gas pedal to start down the hill, Theo's eyes caught two leaping dogs as they chased after a young boy. They were darn-near frolicking through a pumpkin patch.

"Oh, come on! Can't a man just be crabby for two minutes?"

When the dogs caught the boy, they all rolled on the ground. The dogs lapping at the youthful face while the boy laughed hysterically.

Theo couldn't stop the smile. "Okay, fine," he said to himself, accepting the moment with a slight grin. "But just this one. You have brooding to do. And all this happy sappy stuff isn't going to send the right message to people. Especially the women."

Seeing as he'd written women off, he figured the best way to go about this next phase of his life was to do it completely alone.

Theo's red truck with its rounded, old-style bumpers and fenders chugged into town and stopped with a clank. He threw the shifter into park and let his eyes travel the length of the street.

All of the buildings sat side-by-side. Some were brick, some had white wooden paneling, and some sported a shaker-style exterior that reminded Theo of New England.

He climbed out of his truck and stretched his muscles from sitting through the three-hour drive. It wasn't long, but the distance was enough to give him some breathing room and his mind some wide-open space. Not to mention the size of the small town. With a single stretch of main street, a short winding road that led to the water's edge, and only a thousand people that populated it, he figured he'd be safe enough.

Looking around, Theo noticed a diner, a coffee shop, a few outfitters, a book store, and a grocery store at first glance.

It had just about everything a man could ever need when embarking on a new journey. He breathed one more bracing breath, then zeroed in on the coffee shop. Witches' Brew.

Clever.

Theo appreciated the name. And after his initial analysis of the town, it fit perfectly. These people sure had an affinity for fall, what with the decorations on every doorstep and window. He wasn't sure he'd ever seen more pumpkins, broomsticks, or hay bales in his entire life. And his mom had been one of those decorating nut-jobs when he was growing up.

Theo walked toward the glorious scent of coffee. In fact, it nearly pulled him there. Had ground espresso ever smelled so delicious?

The scent dragged him to the door. In a trance, he pulled it open and stepped inside.

The shop was quaint. It had mismatched tables and chairs that somehow all fit together. The walls were stained a deep brown, and the floor was a simple brick pattern that seemed rustic, not by design but by age.

As his eyes traveled to the front of the shop, he watched an old woman who was grinning ear to ear rush away from the counter. If he hadn't stepped out of the way, she very well could have barreled him over on her way out of the door.

Theo laughed a bit at the humor of the sight, then refocused as something was drawing his attention back to the counter.

Then he saw her.

A wild, red-haired beauty, laughing at her conversation with the other woman behind the bar. When she looked up, their eyes met. Theo noticed hers were piercing green, and just below them, her nose sloped into an alluring pointed end.

His heart hammered, while in his mind warning sirens were blaring and flashing as bright as the misery lights that flashed on the top of his old patrol unit.

Then she spoke, and his emergency flares shot in all directions.

"It's you."

Her voice cast a spell over him. If he didn't get out now, he thought he might never be able to leave.

Theo watched as she thought about making a motion to move forward. This was ridiculous. He didn't know who this woman was, but apparently, she knew him. Maybe Lane Paxton, his old friend, told her about his arrival. It was a small town, he supposed that was possible. But, no matter the reason, he didn't want to be known by her – or any other woman for that matter.

Especially one that looked like she did.

Catching himself – and the woman, given her abrupt halt – by surprise, Theo just shouted, "No! No. Nope. Not gonna do it."

Theo backpedaled while she and the rest of the coffee shop watched his outburst. He tripped as he made his way through the threshold of the building, then said, "No way," before stumbling once more and pushing the door closed with more force than he intended.

Nobody on the inside heard the final No. But they did see the shape of his mouth form the word from the other side of the door before he set his rigid body in a   straight   line   and   turned   to   walk   away.

KEEP THE MAGIC GOING

Do you want more of Alice and Theo's magical love story?

Click the link, or scan below get your copy.
(Hover your phone over the image!)

GET THE PROBLEM WITH LOVE POTIONS

COMING SOON

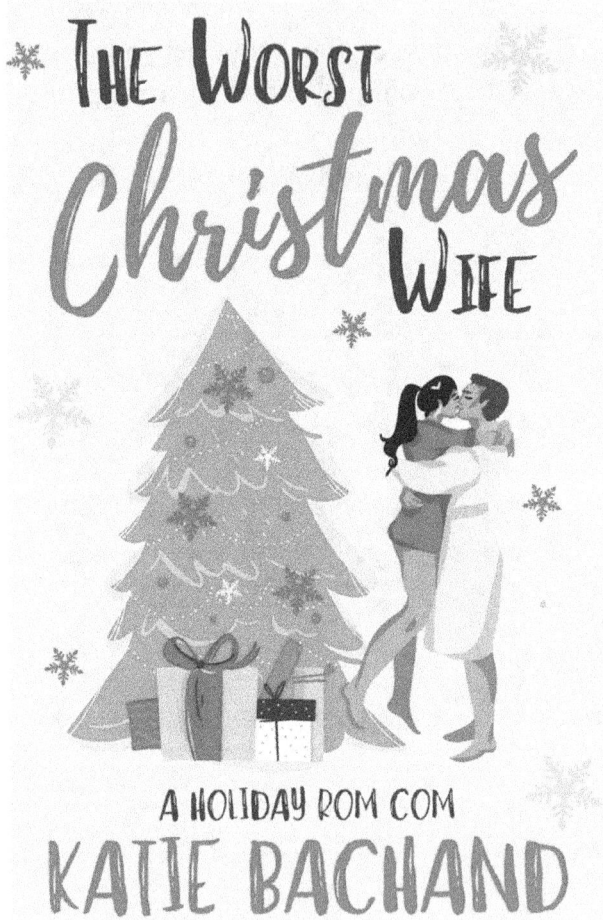

THE WORST
Christmas
WIFE

A HOLIDAY ROM COM
KATIE BACHAND

THE WORST CHRISTMAS WIFE

The Worst Christmas Wife is a laugh-out-lough, holiday rom com about one (extremely handsome) grumpy boss that needs a wife, one over-qualified new assistant that needs a raise and a promotion, and two attracted-to-each-other people who hate that they need each other to make it happen.

Click the link, or scan below get your copy.
(Hover your phone over the image!)

GET THE WORST CHRISTMAS WIFE!

FAVORITE HOLIDAY ROMANCES

WAITING ON CHRISTMAS

Waiting on Christmas is Katie Bachand's best-selling holiday romance. Fall in love this holiday season on a magical Christmas Tree Farm with two people who were destined to be together.

Click the link, or scan below get your copy.
(Hover your phone over the image!)

GET WAITING ON CHRISTMAS!

FAVORITE HOLIDAY ROMANCES

POSTMARK CHRISTMAS

KATIE
BACHAND

POSTMARK CHRISTMAS

Postmark Christmas is Katie Bachand's first sweet, Hallmark-style holiday romance. One, lonely Christmas-lover writes a letter to Santa asking for a magical holiday season. And she gets a reluctant, business-driven man, who has an ulterior motive instead.

Click the link, or scan below get your copy.
(Hover your phone over the image!)

GET POSTMARK CHRISTMAS!

A LAUGH OUT LOUD SERIES

THE TAKING CHANCES SERIES

Head to Katie's website at
www.katiebachandauthor.com
and join her newsletter to get the first book in the
hilarious Taking Chances rom com series for FREE!

Or, simply scan the QR code below.
(Hover your phone camera over the image!)

BOOKS BY KATIE BACHAND

SERIES

Taking Chances Series:
Becoming Us (Prequel)
Conflict of Interest (#1)
In the Business of Love (#2)
A Business Affair (#3)
Betting on Us (#4)

STANDALONES

Romantic Comedy:
The Problem with Love Potions

Christmas Novels:
Postmark Christmas
Waiting on Christmas
A Borrowed Christmas Love Story
The Worst Christmas Wife

ABOUT THE AUTHOR

KATIE BACHAND is the author of contemporary romance, sweet romantic comedy, wholesome holiday romance novels.

KATIE lives with her husband, sons, and golden retriever in beautiful Minneapolis, Minnesota. She hopes in her novels, and in life, you find great friendships, great love, and great appreciation for our wonderful world and the people in it.

Visit Katie on her website at
https://www.katiebachandauthor.com

Or, find Katie on any of your favorite social media outlets by following the link below, or searching **KATIE BACHAND** on Facebook and Instagram.

https://www.instagram.com/katiebachandauthor
https://www.facebook.com/katiebachandauthor

www.ingramcontent.com/pod-product-compliance
Lightning Source LLC
Chambersburg PA
CBHW060523180626
46817CB00002B/466